Jonathan Swift, J. Bowles (John Bowles) Daly

Ireland in the Days of Dean Swift

(Irish Tracts, 1720 to 1734)

Jonathan Swift, J. Bowles (John Bowles) Daly

Ireland in the Days of Dean Swift
(Irish Tracts, 1720 to 1734)

ISBN/EAN: 9783744735292

Printed in Europe, USA, Canada, Australia, Japan

Cover: Foto ©Andreas Hilbeck / pixelio.de

More available books at **www.hansebooks.com**

IRELAND IN THE DAYS OF DEAN SWIFT.

(IRISH TRACTS, 1720 to 1734.)

BY

J. BOWLES DALY, LL.D.

AUTHOR OF "BROKEN IDEALS," "RADICAL PIONEERS OF THE 18TH CENTURY," ETC., ETC.

LONDON—CHAPMAN AND HALL,

LIMITED.

1887.

FORTI NON DEFICIT TELUM

John Watts de Peyster.

TO

The Right Hon. JOHN MORLEY, M.P.,

THE FIRST CHIEF SECRETARY OF IRELAND

WHOSE UNFLINCHING COURAGE AND OUTSPOKEN SYMPATHY

HAS SECURED HIM THE GRATITUDE OF THE IRISH PEOPLE,

THIS BOOK IS DEDICATED

WITH THE ADMIRATION OF

THE AUTHOR.

CONTENTS.

————◆————

		PAGE
INTRODUCTION	. . . .	1
THE DRAPIER'S LETTERS	. .	25
THE ADDRESS TO THE JURY	. . . .	131
SWIFT'S DESCRIPTION OF QUILCA	. .	137
ANSWER TO A PAPER	. . . .	142
MAXIMS CONTROLLED	. . . .	151
A SHORT VIEW OF THE STATE OF IRELAND, 1727 . .	162
THE STORY OF THE INJURED LADY	174
THE ANSWER TO THE INJURED LADY	184
A LETTER TO THE ARCHBISHOP OF DUBLIN, CONCERNING THE WEAVERS.	187
TWO LETTERS ON SUBJECTS RELATIVE TO THE IMPROVEMENT OF IRELAND.	198
THE PRESENT MISERABLE STATE OF IRELAND . .	216
"A PROPOSAL FOR THE UNIVERSAL USE OF IRISH MANUFACTURES." 1720	227
A MODEST PROPOSAL. 1729	240
A CHARACTER, PANEGYRIC, AND DESCRIPTION OF THE LEGION CLUB, 1736	254
ON DOING GOOD	264

IRELAND IN THE DAYS OF DEAN SWIFT.

INTRODUCTION.

THE shifting combinations of party, from the settlement of the constitution at the Revolution to a later period, is an attractive study to any who wish to find the origin of abuses which have long vexed the political life of England. Besides, it is wholesome and instructive to be carried away from the modern difficulty to the broader issues which have gradually led to the present complication.

William III. was a Whig, and his successor a Tory, but except for short periods no Tory party was able in either reign to carry on the government upon Tory principles. William made no complete change of ministry during his reign, only modifying its composition according to what appeared the prevailing sentiment of the parliament or the nation. It was composed of both parties ; the Whigs predominated till the close

B

of the reign, when their opponents acquired ascendency. Anne's first ministry was Tory, but a change was soon wrought by a favourite of the court who happened to be a Whig and who soon turned the scale. Some knowledge of the character of the monarch is indispensable to a clear understanding of the times. In 1702, Anne ascended the throne. The queen's notions of government were those of her family—narrow and despotic. She would have been as arbitrary in her conduct as Elizabeth, but that her actions were restrained by the imbecility of her mind. The queen was the constant slave of favourites who, in their turn, were the tools of intriguing politicians. Events of the greatest importance were crowded into the short space of the twelve years which covered her reign, and the most distinguished intellects adorned the period.

It was because the queen was fascinated by the Duchess of Marlborough that her reign was adorned by the glories of Ramillies and Blenheim : it was because Mrs. Abigail Masham artfully supplanted her benefactress in royal favour, that a stop was put to the war which ravaged the Continent, while by a chambermaid's intrigue Bolingbroke triumphed over his rival, the Earl of Oxford.

During the first part of Anne's reign, Marlborough

was paramount in the Houses of Parliament and his wife in the closet. The Tories came into power on the queen's accession, with Marlborough and Godolphin as leaders. They substantially maintained the policy of King William in prosecuting the war with France, which resulted in making England illustrious in Europe.

Whig principles soon acquired a decided majority in the House, when an act of national importance took place, the. effect of which thrilled the empire. The queen and the duchess quarrelled, and the intriguing waiting-maid stepped into the latter's place. Besides the queen's whims she had a superstitious reverence for the Church; and had been taught to regard the Whigs as Republicans and Dissenters, who wished to subvert the monarchy. Harley traded on this weakness through the instrumentality of Mrs. Masham. This lady was used by him to oust Marlborough and Godolphin, and she continued the tool of Harley and St. John, who now became the chiefs of the new ministry. A jealousy between these two ministers afterwards sprang up, which finally resulted in a quarrel and separation. St. John, created Viscount Bolingbroke, plotted with Mrs. Masham to procure the crown for the Pretender, but the cabal oozed out and alarmed the Tories. The last night of the queen's life was spent in listening to an open quarrel between the waiting-maid and the minister. At two o'clock in the morning she went out of the room to die; she had strength, however, to defeat the schemers by consigning the staff of state to Lord Shrewsbury. "Take it," she said, "for the good of my country." They were the last, perhaps the most pathetic words of her life. When Bolingbroke was defeated, the Whigs came into power and continued in office till the reign of George III.

It was during the reign of William III. that Swift began his political career as a Whig. His patron, Sir William Temple, introduced him to the king, who was so impressed with his talents that he offered to make him a captain of dragoons. Had he accepted this offer, he might have become a second Cromwell. As this distinction was declined, the king promised to see to his future interest. On the death of Temple, Swift edited the works of his patron, dedicated them to the sovereign, and reminded him of his promise. Neither the dedication nor the memorial was noticed. Swift had to fall back on the post of chaplain and private secretary to the Earl of Berkeley, one of the Lords Justices of Ireland. He became a political writer on the side of the Whigs, and associated with

Addison, Steele, and Halifax. From the party leaders he received scores of promises and in the end was neglected. The cup of preferment was twice dashed from his hand ; on the first occasion when Lord Berkeley would have given him a bishopric, his name was vetoed by the Primate on the grounds of his youth, and on the second when he was named for a vacant canonry, but at the last moment the prize was given to another.

During Anne's reign Swift paid frequent visits to England, and became closely connected with the leading Tories. In 1710 he broke with the Whigs and united with Harley and the Tory administration. The five last years of Anne's government found him playing a prominent part in English politics as the leading political writer of the Tories. He was on terms of the closest intimacy with Oxford (Harley) and Bolingbroke, and attempted to heal the breach between the rival statesmen. He helped the Tories in a paper called the *Examiner*, upholding the policy of the ministers and supplying his party with the arguments they would have used if they had had the brains to think of them. This series of articles culminated in the " Conduct of the Allies," a pamphlet which brought about the disgrace of Marlborough and made the peace popular. In it the author denounced the war as the plot of a ring of Whig stock-

jobbers and monied men.   These weekly papers in the
Examiner produced a great effect upon the public mind
and called forth a multitude of opponents.   Swift gave
the Press the wonderful position it holds now. He almost
created the "leading article;" and though his contributions
will not bear comparison with the light style of our own
day, they suited his times.   They were written in a plain,
homely style, for Swift had a thorough contempt for
abstract thought and abstract politics ; indeed, his low
estimate of men convinced him that they were about
as good for flying as for thinking.   Mr. Leslie Stephen
aptly states that Swift's pamphlets were rather "blows
than words ;" he had serious political effects to produce,
and what he had to prove it was necessary to say in
plain words, for honest Tory squires of the country party
to understand and obey.

The *Examiner*, the *Medley*, the *Tattler*, and the
pamphlets of that day bear no analogy to the modern
newspaper ; their influence did not penetrate to the
lower classes of the community, who were still without
education.

Swift is condemned by many who are not conversant
with his character, his writings, or the times in which he
lived.   In detached views, no man was more liable to
be misunderstood ; his individual acts must be compared

with his entire conduct, in order to give him his proper place in the gallery of historical characters. The charge of deserting his party is answered by Dr. Johnson, whose evidence is of greater value as he never professed to be his friend. "Swift, by early education, had been associated with the Whigs; but he deserted them when they deserted their principles, yet he never ran into the opposite extreme; for he continued throughout his life to retain the disposition which he assigned to the Church of England man, of thinking commonly with the Whigs of the State and with the Tories of the Church."

"Swift," say his opponents, "rails at the whole human race;" so he does, and so do we all, at particular times and seasons; when long experience has shown us the selfishness of some, the hollowness of others, and the base ingratitude of the world. Not having lifted his voice in protestation against the terrible penal laws inflicted on his Catholic brethren, and enacted before his door, is, perhaps, the heaviest indictment brought against his name, and the one which, on examination, will prove the most futile. He was the last man who, from his connection with a discarded Tory party, could have taken action with any effect; for if he had made the attempt, and if complaints had originated from it, they would have been interpreted into murmurs of rebellion. One revolt had been put down in Scotland, in which it was supposed that every Catholic in Ireland was implicated, and another which was hatching in the country, broke out in 1745 ; consequently, any interference of Swift on behalf of the Roman Catholics would have drawn upon him the total displeasure of the government and have caused him to be voted an enemy to his country, as was done in the case of Lucas, twenty years after. His words on another occasion show that he was not wanting in sympathy towards the native Irish. "The English should be ashamed of the reproaches they cast on their ignorance, dullness, and want of courage ; defects arising only from the poverty and slavery they suffer from their inhuman neighbours, and the base, corrupt spirit of too many of the gentry. By such treatment as this the very Grecians are grown slavish, ignorant, and superstitious. I do assert that from several experiments I have made in travelling in both England and Ireland, I have found the poor cottagers in the latter kingdom, who could speak our language, to have a much better natural taste for good sense, humour, and raillery than ever I observed among people of the sort in England. But the million of oppressions the national Irish lie under, the tyranny of their landlords, the ridiculous zeal of their priests and the general misery of the whole nation, have been enough to damp the best spirits under the sun."

When Swift's friends were out of power, Oxford no longer at Court and Bolingbroke in exile, he returned to Ireland, and after visiting several parts of the country, and making himself acquainted with the exact condition of the people, he took up the cause of Ireland with a vigour rarely exhibited by any patriot. The last twenty-five years of his sane life were given to his country, during which time he devoted almost all his energy to Irish concerns. His stern sense of justice prompted him to lay bare the wrongs of his native land with the cool calculation of a banker examining accounts, or that of a surgeon cutting open a tumour. His letters, pamphlets, and sermons are full of allusions to the miseries and disabilities of the Irish. In writing to Pope, he disclaims the title of Patriot, and gives us exactly his motive. "What I do," he says, "is owing to perfect rage and resentment, and the mortifying sight of slavery, folly, and baseness about me, among which I am forced to live." It is said that he was a disappointed, mortified man. I allow he was. Swift was ill-used as well as his country. Was he therefore not to resent the injuries offered her because wrongs were heaped on himself, or, after remaining quiet under the disappointments of

years, are we to suppose that at the end of that period
his own private grievances ceased to be intolerable, and
that the public provocations which became urgent had
no effect upon him?

About 1720, a narrow, exclusive clique governed Ireland in avowed contempt of all phases of Irish opinion.
The need of reform had occupied the attention only of
an insignificant handful. None had yet succeeded in
rousing a national spirit to resist the people's wrongs, an
over-insistence of which wrongs was looked upon as
veiled Jacobitism. No doubt Swift's first motive was
opposition to Walpole and his party. He looked back
with bitterness to the fall of his friends. He disliked
the cant of the Whigs and their travesty of liberty; from
that moment his real interest in Ireland began. Swift
scorned Jacobitism, and had a righteous contempt for
"divine right and absolute prerogative." He justified
the Revolution; was opposed to a Popish successor;
had a mortal antipathy to a standing army in time of
peace; desired that parliaments should be annual;
disliked the monied interest in opposition to the terri-
torial; feared the growth of the national debt; and
dreaded further encroachments on the liberty of the
subject. He believed the Whig government of Ireland
to be founded on corruption. All these opinions went

to swell the current of his indignation against Irish
wrongs, and it was in consequence of them that he
lashed the government with his scorpion pen.

The papers written by Swift during the years 1720
to 1734 are now little studied by the people or their
representatives ; nevertheless, if carefully examined,
they will be found useful in throwing light upon
the unsolved problem. They deal with everything
connected with the country : with banks, currency,
agriculture, fisheries, grazing, beggars, planting, bog-re-
claiming and road-making; and all in a style peculiarly
his own, a style seldom equalled and never surpassed.
His pictures of the state of the country present curious
parallels to what we find to-day. There are, of course,
references to grievances which have long ceased to exist ;
such as the penal laws, and the restriction on trade, but
there are many long-standing evils which are not much
better now than they were in Swift's day. The rack-
renting, absentee landlords are more numerous in 1887
than they were in 1730, while the improvements effected
by the tenants were as much a dead loss of capital in the
time of Swift, as in the days of Gladstone.

The secret of Swift's forcible utterances is that he in-
fused himself into everything he wrote ; and his writings,
in consequence, exhibit, not merely his intellectual

power, but also his moral nature, his principles, his pre-judices, even his temper. Swift possessed the most masculine intellect of his age, and was the most earnest thinker of his times. He wrote like a man of the world, and a gentleman ; scorning the conceits of rhetorical flourish, and never stooping to *ad misericordiam* appeals for sympathy.

Of all writers of the English language, his style most approximates to that of the old orators of Greece in force, rapidity, directness, dexterity, luminous statement, and honest homeliness. The reader is impelled with his vigour, as a soldier by the blast of a trumpet ; while his feelings are captivated by his author's manifest sincerity ; his outburst of derisive scorn and withering invective, alternately heat and chill the blood. Perhaps his merit is most revealed in the profound sagacity of his political observations, infusing into his country that spirit which enabled her to demand those rights she at last established. Swift's character rose in Ireland with his defence of it in 1724 ; for, by his conduct then, he acquired an esteem and influence which can never be for-gotten. The question of consideration at that day was not whether Wood's halfpence were good or bad :—the question was, whether an enterprising manufacturer of copper should prevail against Ireland. An insulting

patent, obtained in the most insidious way, was issued by
the British Cabinet without consulting the legitimate
rulers of the country. Against it the grand juries protested,
the corporations protested, the Irish parliament protested.
All failed. At last there stood forth a private clergyman, whose party was proscribed and himself persecuted,
and he carried the country at his back and forced the
British minister to retire within his trenches. Ireland,
trampled on by a British minister, by a British and Irish
parliament ; Ireland that had lost her trade, her judica-
ture, her parliament ; sunk with the weight of oppression,
prevails under the direction of a solitary priest, who not
only inspired but instructed his countrymen in a magnificent vindication of their liberty and the most noble
repudiation of dependence ever taught a nation ; telling
them, "that by the law of God, of nature, of nations, and
of their country they are and ought to be as free a people as their brethren in England."

The patriot rose above the divine. He taught his
country to protest against her grievances, and gave her
a spirit by which she redressed them. Besides, he created
a public opinion in "a nation of slaves" and used it as a
political force against a vicious system of government.
" For my own part," says Swift, referring to the imposition of the copper coinage, "who am but a man of

obscure condition, I do solemnly declare in the presence
of Almighty God that I will suffer the most ignominious
torturing death, rather than submit to receive this accursed
coin, or any other that shall be liable to these objections,
until they shall be forced upon me by a law of my own
country, and if that shall ever happen, I will transport
myself into some foreign land, and eat the bread of
poverty among a free people."

And who was this man who touched with fire the
hearts of a nation and played on their feelings as a skilful musician runs his fingers over the keys of an instrument? A simple journalist, of obscure origin, without
rank or station, with nothing but a beggarly Irish living
to fall back upon, yet endowed with heaven-born genius
and the pride of an insulted god. He treated art like
man : with the same sovereign pride scribbling his
articles in haste, scorning the wretched necessity for reading them over, putting his name to nothing he wrote ;
letting every piece make its way on its own merits, recommended by none. Swift had the soul of a dictator
and the heart of a woman.

This self-devouring heart could not understand
the callousness and indifference of the world. He
asked : "Do not the corruptions and villainies of
men eat your flesh and consume your spirits?"

Swift, like his great Master, was moved by compassion for the multitude. He knew what poverty and scorn were, even at an age when the mind expands and the path of life is sown with generous hopes. At that time, his career was crushed with the iron ring of poverty; maintained by the alms of his family; secretary to a flattered, gouty courtier, at the magnificent salary of 20*l.* a year, and a seat at the servants' table : obliged to submit to the whims of my lord and the fancies of an acidulous virgin, my lord's sister ; lured with false hopes ; and forced, after an attempt at independence, to resume the livery which scorched his soul. When writing his directions to servants, he was relating with bitterness what he himself had suffered ; his proud heart bursting at the memory of indignities received while his lips were locked. Under an outward calm, a tempest of wrath and desire lashed his soul. Twenty years of insult and humiliation, the inner tempest raging, as all his brilliant dreams faded from hope deferred ;—such was the man who moved his country to its centre and won her eternal gratitude.

In discussing the burning topics of the day, Swift had against him the king, his parliament, and all the people of England, together with the Irish government and the Irish judges. The Irish parliament, whose cause he

defended, could not have saved him : that sycophant
assembly could not save itself, and was besides so lowered
and debased by the over-ruling power of England, that it
was more likely to become his prosecutor than his protector.   Swift stood like Atlas, unmoved, and so laid the
foundation of his country's liberty.

" Swift was honoured," says Johnson, " by the popu-
lace of Ireland as their champion, patron, and
instructor, and gained such power as, considered both
in its extent and duration, scarce any man has ever
enjoyed without greater wealth or higher station.   The
benefit was indeed great.   He had rescued Ireland from
a very oppressive and predatory invasion : and the
popularity which he had gained he was very diligent to
keep, by appearing forward and zealous on every
occasion when the public interest was supposed to be
involved.   He showed clearly that wit, confederated
with truth, had such fire as authority was not able to
resist.   He said truly of himself that Ireland was his
debtor.   It was from this time, when he first began to
patronize the Irish, that they may date their riches and
prosperity.   He taught them first to know their own
interest, their weight and their strength; and gave them
spirit to assert that equality with their fellow-subjects,
to which they have ever since been making vigorous

advances, and to claim those rights which they have at last established. Nor can they be charged with ingratitude to their benefactor, for they reverenced him as a guardian and obeyed him as a dictator."

The birth of political and patriotic spirit in Ireland may be traced to the "Drapier's Letters." No agitation that has since taken place in the country has been so immediately and completely successful. The whole power of the English government was found ineffectual to cope with the opposition that had been roused, and marshalled by one man. The Letters brought Swift fame and influence, and from the date of their publication, he became the most powerful and popular man in Ireland. The Irish obeyed his words as if they were the fiat of an oracle.

Swift was no hack writer, lending his pen to any administration that paid for his services ; his individuality placed him above the herd of writers, and he scorned to be used in this way. When Harley sent him a 50*l.* cheque for his first articles in the *Examiner*, he returned it, and haughtily demanded an apology, which was promptly given. He warned the ministers that he acted with them on terms of equality, and that he would not tolerate even coldness on their part ; "for it is what I would hardly bear from a crowned head ; no

C

subject's favour was worth it." He afterwards explained, "If we let these great ministers pretend too much, there will be no governing them."

After the publication of the fourth Drapier's Letter, the government offered a reward for the apprehension of the printer; Swift was so enraged at this proceeding that he suddenly entered the reception-room, elbowed his way up to the Lord-Lieutenant, and, with indignation on his countenance and thunder in his voice, said: "So, my Lord, this is a glorious exploit you performed yesterday in suffering a proclamation against a poor shop-keeper, whose only crime is an honest endeavour to save his country from ruin;" and then added, with a bitter laugh, "I suppose your lordship will expect a statue in copper for your services to Mr. Wood."

The accession of George I. exiled Swift to Ireland, at that time the most impoverished country on the face of the globe. Swift regarded Dublin as a "good enough place to die in." No wonder, when he showed that there were not found in it five gentlemen who could give a dinner at which a scholar and gentleman could find congenial companionship. Ireland then was in a state of national ruin and semi-barbarism; one of the most palpable evils of Irish life was absenteeism. It

was the habit of the English officials elected to remu-
nerative offices, to employ a deputy to perform the duty
on the tenth of the salary—to come over in batches,
landing at Ringsend on Saturday night, receiving the
sacrament at the nearest church on Sunday morning,
taking the oaths on Monday in the Courts, and setting
sail for England in the afternoon, leaving no trace of
their existence in Ireland, save their names on the civil
list as recipients of a salary.

Out of a total rental of 1,800,000*l.* about 600,000*l.* was
spent in England. There was nothing to encourage a
landlord to live in the country ; no political career was
open to him ; all the offices in his country went to
strangers. He was without education or any intellectual interest ; nothing was left him but lavish displays
of brutal luxury, endless carouses, and barbaric hospitality. The Irish landlords were despised for their rude
manners by the fresh importations from England ; they
repaid this contempt on their tenants.

The vast majority of the Catholics were without the
protection of the law ; absolutely ignorant and sunk in
an abyss of poverty. The poor peasant, as soon as the
potatoes were planted, shut up his damp, smoky hut, and
started soliciting alms through the country : idle and lazy,
he wandered from house to house. Begging became a

recognized profession. Adepts were hired to complete
the family group, and these shared the spoils of the
season; girls were debauched, in order that they might, as
fictitious widows, move compassion and earn alms.   In
winter they camped together in companies; the length
and breadth of the country was cursed with a brood of
hedgers, born of adultery and incest, herding together
in troops, when the ties of relationship were as completely lost as in a herd of cattle.

The English clique at the Castle were too much occupied in checking fancied disaffection and dispensing
patronage to secure the support of hungry partisans,
to care for the welfare of the masses.   The local gentry,
despised by the governing clique, allowed matters to
drift from bad to worse.   The better part of the popula-
tion left the country in disgust.   Such was the condition
of Ireland when Swift stood out as its defender.   The
wrongs of Ireland cried to heaven for adjustment.

Since the days of Charles II. the Irish had been forbidden to seek a market in England for their cattle.
Since the last years of William III harsh laws crushed
out the woollen trade, restricting it to a precarious
market formed by a contraband trade with France, every
year getting worse.   Misery wanted only a voice to utter
its lamentation.   Swift assumed this function in his

"Proposal for the universal use of manufactures," published in 1720. Comments on the pamphlets are needless.

The evil of absenteeism was of ancient date and the efforts to eradicate it still older. By a statute of Richard II., two-thirds of the estate of an absentee were forfeited to the Crown. The Lancastrian kings pursued the same policy. Henry VIII. made a strong effort to correct the abuse, by resuming whole Irish estates of some English nobles who were habitual absentees. Under the early Stuarts the same course was pursued, but the evil continues to our own day without any abatement. In Swift's time, residence had not been encouraged ; statutes to enforce it remained on the statute-book, but they were a dead letter. The landlord drew the rent from Ireland, without helping to pay the taxes. He spent it in England and frequently more than the amount, leaving the estates encumbered with mortgages in the hands of English mortgagees. The holder of an Irish office thought only of its emoluments, and was indignant at any suggestion of living in the country burdened with his support, and nominally entitled to his services. The land was reduced to a state of bankruptcy and desolation; famine swept through it, and the people were perishing in thousands. It was at this terrible juncture that Swift put forth in despair his "Modest Proposal," one of the last efforts of his marvellous genius, and it shamed the government into taking some steps to redress the suffering which prevailed.

"Swift's pieces relating to Ireland," says Edmund Burke, "are those of a public nature, in which the Dean appears, as usual, in the best light, because they do honour to his heart as well as his head, furnishing some additional proofs, that though he was very free in his abuse of the inhabitants of that country, as well natives as foreigners, he had their interest sincerely at heart, and perfectly understood it. His sermon on doing good, though peculiarly adapted to Ireland, and Wood's design upon it, contains perhaps the best motives to Patriotism that was ever delivered within so small a compass."

There is no need to refer here to the other works of genius that came from his pen ; they are well known. The object of the present writer is to deal exclusively with what has reference to Ireland, and while exhibiting Swift as a patriot, no attempt is made to exclude his faults or deny his imperfections ; those faults were redeemed by devoted friendship and noble generosity.

His friendship with Addison continued till the day of

his death, and so strong was the bond between them, that when the two met for an evening, they never wished for a third person to support or enliven the conversation. Of him, Pope said :—" Nothing of you can die ; nothing of you can decay; nothing of you can suffer ; nothing of you can be obscured or locked up from esteem and admiration, except what is at the Deanery. May the rest of you be as happy hereafter as honest men may expect and need not doubt, while they know that their Maker is merciful." One can imagine how dear he was to those friends, when Bolingbroke writes :—" I love you for a thousand things, for none more than for the just esteem and love which you have for all the sons of Adam." No one esteemed Swift more than Lord Carteret, who, when hearing of his illness, wrote :—" That you may enjoy the continuation of all happiness is my wish. As to futurity I know your name will be remembered, when the names of Kings, Lord-Lieutenants, Archbishops, and Parliamentary politicians will be forgotten. At last you yourself must fall into oblivion, which may be less than one thousand years, though the term may be uncertain and will depend on the progress that barbarity and ignorance may make, notwithstanding the sedulous endeavours of the great Prelates in this and succeeding ages."

The account of Swift thus coming from men of the greatest genius of their age, carries with it incontestable evidence in his favour, and completely pulverizes the slanderous accusations heaped on him by his enemies. The manly tone of his writing penetrated the character of the whole English colony and bore fruit, long after the proud heart was laid at rest in the great Irish cathedral. The place is marked by an inscription written by himself, and touchingly refers to a time when the heart can no longer be tortured with fierce indignation born from the contemplation of licensed injustice. The character of Swift has long been vindicated, for animosity perishes, but humanity is eternal.

THE DRAPIER'S LETTERS.

THERE was a lack of copper coin in Ireland, which hampered the small transactions of the poor, and rendered the payment of weekly or daily wages a matter of difficulty. This want was reported to the English Cabinet; it was taken up, not as a grievance to be met with redress, but as a new opportunity for a job. A patent to make a copper coinage was granted to William Wood, a gentleman whose antecedents were not creditable. According to the habits of the day, the patent had to pass through various officials, each of whom had doubtless to be paid: a sort of black-mail on the transaction. The amount of the coinage had to be large to enable Wood to recoup himself and make his own profit. It was fixed at 108,000*l.*, a sum vastly in excess of its need. The greatest share of the plunder was to fall to the king's mistress. The Duchess of Kendal was to receive 10,000*l.* from Wood, to whom she farmed the patent. It was from the bottom to the top a scandalous job, and to add to its depravity, it was passed without consulting the responsible governors of the country. It was only when all efforts to defeat its passage were concluded, that Swift stepped in.   The indignation of the country had risen to boiling-point ; he gave it a voice.   In describing the patent, Swift exaggerated its consequences. It is absurd to suppose that what he said of it was absolutely true, or that Swift thought it to be true.   His object was to put a scandalous transaction in the grossest aspect possible.   Swift adopted the ordinary recognized methods of political controversy.   Apart from exaggeration, there was enough of injustice in the matter to justify any language which would tend to remove it.

LETTER I.

To the Tradesmen, Shopkeepers, Farmers, and Country-people in general, of the Kingdom of Ireland,

Concerning the brass halfpence coined by one William Wood, Hardwareman, with a design to have them pass in this kingdom !

Wherein is shewn the power of his Patent, the value of his Halfpence, and how far every person may be obliged to take the same in payments, and how to behave himself, in case such an attempt should be made by Wood, or any other person.

(VERY PROPER TO BE KEPT IN EVERY FAMILY.)

By M. B., DRAPIER, 1724.

BRETHREN, FRIENDS, COUNTRYMEN, AND FELLOW-SUBJECTS.

WHAT I intend now to say to you, is, next to your duty to God, and the care of your salvation, of the greatest concern to yourselves and your children ; your bread and clothing, and every common necessary of life, depend entirely upon it. Therefore I do most earnestly exhort you as men, as Christians, as parents, and as lovers of your country, to read this paper with the utmost attention, or get it read to you by others ; which, that you may do at the less expense, I have ordered the printer to sell it at the lowest rate.

It is a great fault among you, that when a person writes with no other intention than to do you good, you will not be at the pains to read his advices. One copy of this paper may serve a dozen of you, which will be less than a farthing apiece. It is your folly, that you have no common or general interest in your view, not even the wisest among you ; neither do you know, or inquire, or care, who are your friends, or who are your enemies.

About four years ago, a little book was written to advise all people to wear the manufactures of this our own dear country.[1] It had no other design, said nothing against the King or Parliament, or any persons whatever ; yet the poor printer was prosecuted two years with the utmost violence, and even some weavers themselves (for whose sake it was written), being upon the JURY,

[1] See the " Proposal for the Use of Irish Manufactures."

found him guilty.   This would be enough to discourage any man from endeavouring to do you good, when you will either neglect him, or fly in his face for his pains, and when he must expect only danger to himself, and to be fined and imprisoned, perhaps to his ruin.

However, I cannot but warn you once more of the manifest destruction before your eyes, if you do not behave yourself, as you ought.

I will therefore first tell you the plain story of the fact, and then I will lay before you how you ought to act, in common prudence according to the laws of your country.

The fact is this : It having been many years since COPPER HALFPENCE OR FARTHINGS were last coined in this kingdom, they have been for some time very scarce, and many counterfeits passed about under the name of *raps*, several applications were made to England that we might have liberty to coin new ones, as in former times we did ; but they did not succeed.   At last, one Mr. Wood, a mean ordinary man, a hardware dealer, procured a patent under his Majesty's broad seal to coin 108,000*l*.[2] in copper for this kingdom ; which patent, however, did not oblige any one here to take them, unless they pleased.   Now you must know,

---

[2] Four score and ten thousand, this runs throughout the first edition.

that the halfpence and farthings in England pass for
very little more than they are worth ; and if you should
beat them to pieces, and sell them to the brazier, you
would not lose much above a penny in a shilling. But
Mr. Wood made his halfpence of such base metal, and
so much smaller than the English ones, that the brazier
would not give you above a penny of good money for a
shilling of his; so that this sum of 108,000l. in good
gold and silver, must be given for trash, that will not be
worth eight or nine thousand pounds real value. But
this is not the worst ; for Mr. Wood, when he pleases,
may, by stealth, send over another 108,000l., and buy
all our goods for eleven parts in twelve under the value.
For example, if a hatter sells a dozen of hats for five
shillings apiece, which amounts to three pounds, and
receives the payment in Wood's coin, he really receives
only the value of five shillings.

Perhaps you will wonder how such an ordinary fellow
as this Mr. Wood could have so much interest as to
get his Majesty's broad seal for so great a sum of bad
money to be sent to this poor country ; and that all the
nobility and gentry here could not obtain the same
favour, and let us make our own halfpence, as we used
to do. Now I will make that matter very plain : We
are at a great distance from the King's court, and have

nobody there to solicit for us, although a great number of lords and 'squires, whose estates are here, and are our countrymen, spend all their lives and fortunes there; but this same Mr. Wood was able to attend constantly for his own interest; he is an Englishman, and had great friends; and, it seems, knew very well where to give money to those that would speak to others, that could speak to the King, and would tell a fair story. And his Majesty, and perhaps the great lord or lords who advise him, might think it was for our country's good; and so, as the lawyers express it, "The King was deceived in his grant," which often happens in all reigns. And I am sure if his Majesty knew that such a patent, if it should take effect according to the desire of Mr. Wood, would utterly ruin this kingdom, which has given such great proofs of its loyalty, he would immediately recall it, and perhaps show his displeasure to somebody or other; but a word to the wise is enough. Most of you must have heard with what anger our honourable House of Commons received an account of this Wood's patent. There were several fine speeches made upon it, and plain proofs that it was all a wicked cheat from the bottom to the top; and several smart votes were printed, which that same Wood had the assurance to answer likewise in print; and in so confident a way, as if he were a better man than our whole Parliament put together.

This Wood, as soon as his patent was passed, or soon after, sends over a great many barrels of those halfpence to Cork, and other seaport towns; and to get them off, offered a hundred pounds in his coin, for seventy or eighty in silver; but the collectors of the King's customs very honestly refused to take them, and so did almost everybody else. And since the Parliament has condemned them, and desired the King that they might be stopped, all the kingdom do abominate them.

But Wood is still working underhand to force his halfpence upon us; and if he can, by the help of his friends in England, prevail so far as to get an order, that the commissioners and collectors of the King's money shall receive them, and that the army is to be paid with them, then he thinks his work shall be done. And this is the difficulty you will be under in such a case: for the common soldier, when he goes to the market, or ale-house, will offer this money; and if it be refused, perhaps he will swagger and hector, and threaten to beat the butcher or ale-wife, or take the goods by force, and throw them the bad halfpence. In this and the like cases, the shopkeeper or victualler, or any other tradesman, has no more to do, than to demand ten times the price of his goods, if it is to be paid in Wood's money; for example, twenty pence of that money for a quart of ale and so in all things else, and not part with his goods till he gets the money.

For, suppose you go to an ale-house with that base money, and the landlord gives you a quart for four of those halfpence, what must the victualler do? his brewer will not be paid in that coin; or, if the brewer should be such a fool, the farmers will not take it from them for their bere,[3] because they are bound, by their leases, to pay their rent in good and lawful money of England; which this is not, nor of Ireland neither; and the 'squire, their landlord, will never be so bewitched to take such trash for his land; so that it must certainly stop somewhere or other; and wherever it stops, it is the same thing, and we are all undone.

The common weight of these halfpence is between four and five to an ounce—suppose five, then three shillings and four pence will weigh a pound, and consequently twenty shillings will weigh six pounds butter weight. Now there are many hundred farmers, who pay two hundred pounds a-year rent; therefore, when one of these farmers comes with his half-year's rent, which is one hundred pounds, it will be at least

[3] A coarse kind of barley.

six hundred pounds' weight, which is three horses' load.

If a 'squire has a mind to come to town to buy clothes and wine, and spices for himself and family, or perhaps to pass the winter here, he must bring with him five or six horses well loaden with sacks, as the farmers bring their corn ; and when his lady comes in her coach to our shops, it must be followed by a car loaded with Mr. Wood's money. And I hope we shall have the grace to take it for no more than it is worth.

They say 'Squire Conolly[4] has sixteen thousand pounds a-year ; now, if he sends for his rent to town, as it is likely he does, he must have two hundred and fifty horses to bring up his half-year's rent, and two or three great cellars in his house for stowage. But what the bankers will do I cannot tell ; for I am assured, that some great bankers keep by them forty thousand pounds in ready cash, to answer all payments ; which sum, in Mr. Wood's money, would require twelve hundred horses to carry it.

For my own part, I am already resolved what to do ; I have a pretty good shop of Irish stuffs and silks ; and instead of taking Mr. Wood's bad copper, I intend to truck with my neighbours, the butchers, and bakers, and

[4] At that time the Speaker of the Irish House of Commons.

D

brewers, and the rest, goods for goods ; and the little
gold and silver I have, I will keep by me, like my heart's
blood, till better times, or until I am just ready to starve ;
and then I will buy Mr. Wood's money, as my father
did the brass money in King James's time,[5] who could
buy ten pounds of it with a guinea ; and I hope to get
as much for a pistole, and so purchase bread from those
who will be such fools as to sell it me.   These halfpence,
if they once pass, will soon be counterfeited, because it
may be cheaply done, the stuff is so base.   The Dutch,
likewise, will probably do the same thing, and send
them over to us to pay for our goods ; and Mr. Wood
will never be at rest, but coin on : so that in some years
we shall have at least five times 108,000*l.* of this lumber.
Now the current money of this kingdom is not reckoned
to be above four hundred thousand pounds in all; and
while there is a silver sixpence left, these blood-suckers
will never be quiet.   When once the kingdom is reduced
to such a condition, I will tell you what must be the
end : the gentlemen of estates will all turn off their
tenants for want of payments, because, as I told you
before, the tenants are obliged by their leases to pay
sterling, which is lawful current money of England ;

---

[5] An allusion to the debasement of the coin by James II. during
his unfortunate campaign in Ireland.

then they will turn their own farmers, as too many of
them do already, run all into sheep, where they can,
keeping only such other cattle as are necessary ; then
they will be their own merchants, and send their wool,
and butter, and hides, and linen beyond sea, for ready
money, and wine, and spices, and silks. They will keep
only a few miserable cottagers ; the farmers must rob,
or beg, or leave their country ; the shopkeepers in this,
and every other town, must break and starve ; for it is
the landed man that maintains the merchant, and shopkeeper, and handicraftsman.

But when the 'squire turns farmer and merchant himself, all the good money he gets from abroad he will
hoard up to send for England, and keep some poor
tailor or weaver and the like in his own house, who will
be glad to get bread at any rate.

I should never have done, if I were to tell you all the
miseries that we shall undergo, if we be so foolish and
wicked as to take this cursed coin. It would be very
hard if all Ireland should be put into one scale, and this
sorry fellow, Wood, into the other ; that Mr. Wood
should weigh down this whole kingdom, by which
England gets above a million of good money every year
clear into their pockets ; and that is more than the
English do by all the world besides.

But your great comfort is, that as his Majesty's patent
does not oblige you to take this money, so the laws have
not given the crown a power of forcing the subject to
take what money the King pleases ; for then, by the
same reason, we might be bound to take pebble-stones,
or cockle-shells, or stamped leather, for current coin, if
ever we should happen to live under an ill prince ; who
might likewise, by the same power, make a guinea pass
for ten pounds, a shilling for twenty shillings, and so
on ; by which he would, in a short time, get all the
silver and gold of the kingdom into his own hands, and
leave us nothing but brass or leather, or what he pleased.
Neither is anything reckoned more cruel and oppressive
in the French government than their common practice
of calling in all their money, after they have sunk it very
low, and then coining it anew at a much higher value ;
which, however, is not the thousandth part so wicked
as this abominable project of Mr. Wood. For the
French give their subjects silver for silver, and gold for
gold ; but this fellow will not so much as give us good
brass or copper for our gold and silver, nor even a
twelfth part of their worth. Having said thus much, I
will now go on to tell you the judgment of some great
lawyers in this matter, whom I fee'd on purpose for your
sakes, and got their opinions under their hands, that I

might be sure I went upon good grounds. . . . . I will now, my dear friends, to save you the trouble, set before you, in short, what the law obliges you to do, and what it does not oblige you to.

First, you are obliged to take all money in payments which is coined by the King, and is of the English standard or weight, provided it be of gold or silver.

Secondly, you are not obliged to take any money which is not of gold or silver; not only the halfpence or farthings of England, but of any other country. And it is merely for convenience or ease, that you are content to take them; because the custom of coining silver halfpence and farthings has long been left off; I suppose on account of their being subject to be lost.

Thirdly, much less are you obliged to take those vile halfpence of the same Wood, by which you must lose almost eleven pence in every shilling. Therefore, my friends, stand to it one and all; refuse this filthy trash. It is no treason to rebel against Mr. Wood. His Majesty in his patent, obliges nobody to take these halfpence, our gracious prince has no such ill-advisers about him; or, if he had, yet you see the laws have not left it in the King's power to force us to take any coin but what is lawful, of right standard, gold and silver. Therefore you have nothing to fear.

And let me in the next place apply myself particularly to you who are the poorer sort of tradesmen. Perhaps you may think you will not be so great losers as the rich, if these halfpence should pass ; because you seldom see any silver, and your customers come to your shops or stalls with nothing but brass, which you likewise find hard to be got. But you may take my word, whenever this money gains footing among you, you will be utterly undone. If you carry these halfpence to a shop for tobacco or brandy, or any other thing that you want, the shopkeeper will advance his goods accordingly, or else he must break, and leave the key under the door. " Do you think I will sell you a yard of tenpenny stuff for twenty of Mr. Wood's halfpence ? No, not under two hundred at least; neither will I be at the trouble of counting, but weigh them in a lump." I will tell you one thing farther, that if Mr. Wood's project should take, it would ruin even our beggars ; for when I give a beggar a halfpenny, it will quench his thirst, or go a good way to fill his belly ; but the twelfth part of a halfpenny will do him no more service than if I should give him three pins out of my sleeve.

In short, these halfpence are like " the accursed thing, which," as the Scripture tells us, " the children of Israel were forbidden to touch." They will run about like the

plague, and destroy every one who lays his hand upon
them. I have heard scholars talk of a man who
told the King, that he had invented a way to torment people, by putting them into a bull of brass
with fire under it ; but the prince put the projector first
into it, to make the experiment. This very much resembles the project of Mr. Wood ; and the like of this
may probably be Mr. Wood's fate ; that the brass he
contrived to torment this kingdom with, may prove his
own torment, and his destruction at last.

N.B. The author of this paper is informed by
persons, who have made it their business to be exact in
their observations on the true value of these halfpence,
that any person may expect to get a quart of twopenny
ale for thirty-six of them.

I desire that all families may keep this paper carefully
by them, to refresh their memories whenever they shall
have farther notice of Mr. Wood's halfpence, or any other
the like imposture.

SECOND LETTER.

WALPOLE recommended his Majesty to compromise
the grave issue which had risen. An order was issued
restricting the importation of Wood's copper coin to

the sum of 40,000*l.* instead of 108,000*l.*, to be current only amongst those who should be willing to accept them. But the dispute had risen too high to admit of accommodation. The real grievance of this measure lay rather in its principle than its immediate effects. The merits and details of the question are now laid aside. Even Wood is almost forgotten in the vehemence of rage, that a nation should be exposed to the menaces or mercies of such an adventurer.

LETTER II.

To Mr. Harding, the Printer,

On occasion of a paragraph in his newspaper of August 1, 1724, relating to Mr. Wood's halfpence.

August 4, 1724.

IN your Newsletter of the first instant, there is a paragraph, dated from London, July 25, relating to Wood's halfpence; whereby it is plain, what I foretold in my letter to the shopkeepers, &c., that this vile fellow would never be at rest; and that the danger of our ruin approaches nearer; and therefore the kingdom requires new and fresh warning. However, I take this paragraph to be, in a great measure, an imposition upon the public; at least I hope so, because I am informed

that Mr. Wood is generally his own newswriter. I
cannot but observe from that paragraph, that this
public enemy of ours, not satisfied to ruin us with his
trash, takes every occasion to treat this kingdom with
the utmost contempt. He represents several of our
merchants and traders, upon examination before a
committee of council, agreeing, that there was the
utmost necessity of copper money here, before his
patent; so that several gentlemen have been forced to
tally with their workmen, and give them bits of cards
sealed and subscribed with their names. What then?
If a physician prescribe to a patient a dram of physic,
shall a rascal apothecary cram him with a pound, and
mix it up with poison? And is not a landlord's hand
and seal to his own labourers a better security for five
or ten shillings, than Wood's brass, ten times below the
real value, can be to the kingdom for a hundred and
eight thousand pounds?

Who are these merchants and traders of Ireland that
made this report of the utmost necessity we are under
for copper money? They are only a few betrayers of
their country, confederates with Wood, from whom they
are to purchase a great quantity of coin, perhaps at half
the price that we are to take it, and vend it among us to
the ruin of the public, and their own private advantages.

Are not these excellent witnesses, upon whose integrity the fate of the kingdom must depend, evidences in their own cause, and sharers in this work of iniquity?

If we could have deserved the liberty of coining for ourselves as we formerly did—and why we have it not is everybody's wonder as well as mine—ten thousand pounds might have been coined here in Dublin of only one-fifth below the intrinsic value, and this sum, with the stock of halfpence we then had, would have been sufficient. But Wood, by his emissaries—enemies to God and this kingdom—has taken care to buy up as many of our old halfpence as he could, and from thence the present want of change arises; to remove which, by Mr. Wood's remedy, would be to cure a scratch on the finger by cutting off the arm. But, supposing there were not one farthing of change in the whole nation, I will maintain that five-and-twenty thousand pounds would be a sum fully sufficient to answer all our occasions I am no inconsiderable shopkeeper in this town. I have discoursed with several of my own and other trades, with many gentlemen both of city and country, and also with great numbers of farmers, cottagers, and labourers, who all agree that two shillings in change for every family would be more than necessary in all dealings. Now, by the largest computation—even before that grievous discouragement of agriculture, which has so much lessened our numbers—the souls in 'this kingdom are computed to be one million and a half; which allowing six to a family, makes two hundred and fifty thousand families, and, consequently, two shillings to each family will amount only to five-and-twenty thousand pounds ; whereas this honest, liberal hardwareman, Wood, would impose upon us above four times that sum. Your paragraph relates further, that Sir Isaac Newton reported an assay taken at the Tower of Wood's metal, by which it appears, that Wood had in all respects performed his contract. His contract !— With whom ? Was it with the Parliament or people of Ireland ? Are not they to be the purchasers ? But they detest, abhor, and reject it, as corrupt, fraudulent, mingled with dirt and trash. Upon which he grows angry, goes to law, and will impose his goods upon us by force.

But your newsletter says, that an assay was made of the coin. How impudent and insupportable is this ! Wood takes care to coin a dozen or two halfpence of good metal, sends them to the Tower, and they are approved ; and these must answer all that he has already coined, or shall coin for the future. It is true, indeed, that a gentleman often sends to my shop for a pattern of stuff; I cut it fairly off, and, if he likes it, he comes, or sends, and compares the pattern with the whole piece, and probably we come to a bargain. But if I were to buy a hundred sheep, and the grazier should bring me one single wether, fat and well-fleeced, by way of pattern, and expect the same price round for the whole hundred, without suffering me to see them before he was paid, or giving me good security to restore my money for those that were lean, or shorn, or scabby, I would be none of his customer. I have heard of a man who had a mind to sell his house, and therefore carried a piece of brick in his pocket, which he showed as a pattern to encourage purchasers; and this is directly the case in point with Mr. Wood's assay.

The next part of the paragraph contains Mr. Wood's voluntary proposals for preventing any further objections or apprehensions.

His first proposal is, "That whereas he has already coined seventeen thousand pounds, and has copper prepared to make it up forty thousand pounds, he will be content to coin no more, unless the EXIGENCIES OF TRADE REQUIRE IT, although his patent empowers him to coin a far greater quantity."

To which if I were to answer, it should be thus:—
" Let Mr. Wood, and his crew of founders and tinkers

coin on, till there is not an old kettle left in the kingdom, —let them coin old leather, tobacco-pipe clay, or the dirt in the street, and call their trumpery by what name they please, from a guinea to a farthing,—we are not under concern to know how he and his tribe of accomplices think fit to employ themselves. But I hope and trust, that we are all to a man fully determined to have nothing to do with him or his ware."

The King has given him a patent to coin halfpence, but has not obliged us to take them; and I have already shown, in my letter to the shopkeepers, &c., that the law has not left it in the power of the prerogative to compel the subject to take any money besides gold and silver, of the right sterling and standard.

Wood further proposes, if I understand him right— for his expressions are dubious—that he will not coin above forty thousand pounds, unless the exigencies of trade require it.

First, I observe, that this sum of forty thousand pounds is almost double to what I proved to be sufficient for the whole kingdom, although we had not one of our old halfpence left.

Again, I ask, who is to be judge when the exigencies of trade require it? Without doubt he means himself; for as to us of this poor kingdom, who must be utterly

ruined if this project should succeed, we were never once
consulted till the matter was over, and he will judge of
our exigencies by his own. Neither will these ever be
at an end till he and his accomplices think they have
enough ; and it now appears, that he will not be content with all our gold and silver, but intends to buy up
our goods and manufactures with the same coin. . . .
His last proposal, being of a peculiar strain and nature,
deserves to be very particularly considered, both on
account of the matter and · the style. It is as
follows :—

" Lastly, in consideration of the direful apprehensions
which prevail in Ireland, that Mr. Wood will, by such
coinage, drain them of their gold and silver, he proposes
to take their manufactures in exchange, and that no
person be obliged to receive more than fivepence halfpenny at one payment."

First, observe this little impudent hardwareman turning into ridicule the direful apprehensions of a whole kingdom, priding himself as the cause of them, and daring
to prescribe what no King of England ever attempted,
how far a whole nation shall be obliged to take his
brass coin. And he has reason to insult; for sure
there was never an example in history of a great kingdom kept in awe for above a year, in daily dread of

utter destruction—not by a powerful invader, at the head of twenty thousand men—not by a plague or a famine—not by a tyrannical prince (for we never had one more gracious), or a corrupt administration—but by one single, diminutive, insignificant mechanic. . . . . His proposals conclude with perfect high treason. He promises, that no person shall be obliged to receive more than fivepence halfpenny of his coin in one payment. By which it is plain, that he pretends to oblige every subject in this kingdom to take so much in every payment if it be offered; whereas his patent obliges no man, nor can the prerogative, by law, claim such a power, as I have often observed; so that here Mr. Wood takes upon him the entire legislature, and an absolute dominion over the properties of the whole nation.

Good God! who are this wretch's advisers? Who are his supporters, abettors, encouragers, or sharers? Mr. Wood will oblige me to take fivepence halfpenny of his brass in every payment; and I will shoot Mr. Wood and his deputies through the head, like highwaymen or housebreakers, if they dare to force one farthing of their coin on me in the payment of a hundred pounds. It is no loss of honour to submit it to the lion; but who, with the figure of a man, can think with patience of

being devoured alive by a rat ?   He has laid a tax upon
the people of Ireland of seventeen shillings, at least, in
the pound ; a tax, I say, not only upon lands, but
interest-money, goods, manufactures, the hire of handi-
craftsmen, labourers, and servants.

Shopkeepers, look to yourselves !—Wood will oblige
and force you to take fivepence halfpenny of his trash
in every payment, and many of you receive twenty,
thirty, forty payments in one day, or else you can
hardly find bread.   And, pray, consider how much that
will amount to in a year.   Twenty times fivepence halfpenny is nine shillings and twopence, which is above a
hundred and sixty pounds a year ; wherein you will be
losers of at least one hundred and forty pounds by
taking your payments in his money.   If any of you be
content to deal with Mr. Wood on such conditions, you
may ; but, for my own particular, let his money perish
with him ! If the famous Mr. Hampden rather chose to go
to prison than pay a few shillings to King Charles I. without authority of Parliament, I will rather choose to be
hanged than have all my substance taxed at seventeen
shillings in the pound, at the arbitrary will and pleasure
of the venerable Mr. Wood.

The paragraph concludes thus :—" N.B." that is to
say, *nota bene*, or *mark well*, " No evidence appeared

from Ireland, or elsewhere, to prove the mischiefs complained of, or any abuses whatsoever committed, in the execution of the said grant."

The impudence of this remark exceeds all that went before. First, the House of Commons in Ireland, which represents the whole people of the kingdom, and, secondly, the Privy-council, addressed his Majesty against these halfpence. What could be done more to express the universal sense of the nation? If his copper were diamonds, and the kingdom were entirely against it, would not that be sufficient to reject it? Must a committee of the whole House of Commons, and our whole Privy-council, go over to argue *pro* and *con* with Mr. Wood? To what end did the King give his patent for coining halfpence for Ireland? Was it not because it was represented to his sacred Majesty, that such a coinage would be of advantage to the good of this kingdom, and of all his subjects here? It is to the patentee's peril if this representation be false, and the execution of his patent be fraudulent and corrupt. Is he so wicked and foolish to think, that his patent was given him to ruin a million and a half of people, that he might be a gainer of three or four score thousand pounds to himself? Before he was at the charge of passing a patent, much more of raking up so

E

much filthy dross, and stamping it with his Majesty's image and superscription, should he not first, in common sense, in common equity, and common manners, have consulted the principal party concerned,—that is to say, the people of the kingdom, the House of Lords, or Commons, or the Privy-council? If any foreigner should ask us, whose image and superscription there is on Wood's coin? we should be ashamed to tell him it was Cæsar's. In that great want of copper halfpence which he alleges we were, our city set up our Cæsar's statue [6] in excellent copper, at an expense that is equal to thirty thousand pounds of his coin, and we will not receive his image in worse metal.

I observe many of our people putting a melancholy case on this subject. "It is true," say they, "we are all undone if Wood's halfpence must pass; but what shall we do if his Majesty puts out a proclamation, commanding us to take them? This has often been dinned in my ears; but I desire my countrymen to be assured that there is nothing in it. The King never issues out a proclamation but to enjoin what the law permits him. He will not issue out a proclamation against law; or, if such a thing should happen by a mistake, we are no

[6] An equestrian statue of George I. at Essex Bridge, Dublin.

more obliged to obey it, than to run our heads into the fire.

Besides, his Majesty will never command us by a proclamation, what he does not offer to command us in the patent itself.

There he leaves it to our discretion, so that our destruction must be entirely owing to ourselves; therefore, let no man be afraid of a proclamation which will never be granted, and if it should, yet, upon this occasion, will be of no force.

The King's revenues here are near four hundred thousand pounds a-year. Can you think his ministers will advise him to take them in Wood's brass, which will reduce the value to fifty thousand pounds? England gets a million sterling by this nation; which, if this project goes on, will be almost reduced to nothing. And do you think those who live in England upon Irish estates, will be content to take an eight or tenth part by being paid in Wood's dross?

If Wood and his confederates were not convinced of our stupidity, they never would have attempted so audacious an enterprise. He now sees a spirit has been raised against him, and he only watches till it begin to flag: he goes about watching when to devour us. He hopes we shall be weary of contending with him; and

at last, out of ignorance or fear, or of being perfectly tired
with opposition, we shall be forced to yield ; and therefore, I confess, it is my chief endeavour to keep up your
spirits and resentments.   If I tell you, " there is a preci-
pice under you, and that if you go forward you will
certainly break your necks ;" if I point to it before your
eyes, must I be at the trouble of repeating it every
morning ?   Are our people's hearts waxed gross ?   Are
their ears dull of hearing ?   And have they closed their
eyes ?   I fear there are some few vipers among us, who
for ten or twenty pounds' gain would sell all their souls
and their country ; although at last it should end in their
own ruin, as well as ours.   Be not like " the deaf adder,
who refuseth to hear the voice of the charmer, charm he
never so wisely."

Although my letter be directed to you, Mr. Harding,
yet I intend it for all my countrymen.   I have no
interest in this affair, but what is common to the public.
I can live better than many others ; I have some gold
and silver by me, and a shop well furnished : and shall
be able to make a shift when many of my betters are
starving.   But I am grieved to see the coldness and
indifference of many people with whom I discourse.
Some are afraid of a proclamation ; others shrug up their
shoulders, and cry, " What would you have us to do ?"

Some give out there is no danger at all ; others are comforted, that it will be a common calamity, and they shall fare no worse than their neighbours. Will a man who hears midnight robbers at his door, get out of bed, and raise his whole family for a common defence; and shall a whole kingdom lie in a lethargy, while Mr. Wood comes, at the head of his confederates, to rob them of all they have, to ruin us and our posterity for ever? If a highwayman meets you on the road, you give him your money to save your life ; but, God be thanked, Mr. Wood cannot touch a hair of your heads. You have all the laws of God and man on your side ; when he or his accomplices offer you his dross, it is but saying no, and you are safe. If a madman should come into my shop with a handful of dirt raked out of the kennel, and offer it in payment for ten yards of stuff, I would pity or laugh at him ; or, if his behaviour deserved it, kick him out of my doors. And if Mr. Wood comes to demand my gold and silver, or commodities for which I have paid my gold and silver, in exchange for his trash, can he deserve or expect better treatment ?

When the evil day is come (if it must come), let us mark and observe those who persevere to offer these halfpence in payment. Let their names and trades, and places of abode, be made public, that every one may be aware of them, as betrayers of their country, and confederates with Mr. Wood. Let them be watched at markets and fairs; and let the first honest discoverer give the word about that Mr. Wood's halfpence have been offered, and caution the poor innocent people not to receive them.

Perhaps I have been too tedious, but there would never be an end if I attempted to say all that this melancholy subject will bear. I will conclude with humbly offering one proposal; which, if it were put into practice, would blow up this destructive project at once. Let some skilful, judicious pen draw up an advertisement to the following purpose :—

"Whereas one William Wood, hardwareman, now or lately sojourning in the city of London, has, by many misrepresentations, procured a patent for coining a hundred and eight thousand pounds in copper halfpence for this kingdom, which is a sum five times greater than our occasions require : And whereas it is notorious, that the said Wood has coined his halfpence of such base metal and false weight, that they are at least six parts in seven below the real value : And whereas we have reason to apprehend, that the said Wood may at any time hereafter clandestinely coin as many more halfpence as he pleases : And whereas the said patent neither does, nor can, oblige his Majesty's subjects to receive the said halfpence in any payment, but leaves it to their voluntary choice; because by law the subject cannot be obliged to take any money, except gold or silver: And whereas, contrary to the letter and meaning of the said patent, the said Wood has declared that every person shall be obliged to take fivepence halfpenny of his coin in every payment: And whereas the House of Commons and Privy-council have severally addressed his most sacred Majesty, representing the ill consequences which the said coinage would have upon this kingdom: And lastly, whereas it is universally agreed, that the whole nation to a man (except Mr. Wood and his confederates) are in the utmost apprehensions of the ruinous consequences that must follow from the said coinage; Therefore, we, whose names are underwritten, being persons of considerable estates in this kingdom, and residers therein, do unanimously resolve and declare, that we will never receive one farthing or halfpenny of the said Wood's coining; and that we will direct all our tenants to refuse the said coin from any person whatsoever; of which, that they may not be ignorant, we have sent them a copy of this advertisement, to be read to them by our stewards, receivers," &c.

I could wish, that a paper of this nature might be

drawn up, and signed by two or three hundred principal gentlemen of this kingdom ; and printed copies thereof sent to their several tenants.   I am deceived if anything could sooner defeat this execrable design of Wood and his accomplices.   This would immediately give the alarm, and set the kingdom on their guard ; this would give courage to the meanest tenant and cottager.

" How long, O Lord, righteous and true," &c.

I must tell you in particular, Mr. Harding, that you are much to blame.   Several hundred persons have inquired at your house for my " Letter to the Shop-keepers," &c., and you had none to sell them.   Pray keep yourself provided with that letter and with this ; you have got very well by the former ; but I did not then write for your sake, any more than I do now. Pray advertise both in every newspaper ; and let it not be your fault or mine, if our countrymen will not take warning.   I desire you likewise to sell them as cheap as you can.

I am your servant,

M. B.

THIRD LETTER.

THE object of this Letter is no longer to argue against a scheme which is universally condemned.   The

independence of Ireland is what he insists on : and the
duty of her leading men is to assert that independence.
In this he assumed a freedom of spirit which did not
really exist. The sketch was skilfully drawn, so as to
prepare men for a new appeal, and was far from being
the last word. Two months after the fourth and greatest
Letter appeared.

LETTER III.

*Some observations on a paper, called, The report of the
committee of the most honourable the Privy-council in
England, relating to Wood's halfpence.*

To the Nobility and Gentry of the Kingdom
of Ireland.

August 25th, 1724.

Having already written two letters to the people of
my own level and condition, and having now very
pressing occasion for writing a third, I thought I could
not more properly address it than to your lordships
and worships.

The occasion is this. A printed paper was sent to
me on the 18th instant, entitled, " A Report of the
Committee of the Lords of his Majesty's Most Honourable Privy-council in England, relating to Mr. Wood's
Halfpence and Farthings."

There is no mention made where the paper was printed, but I suppose it to have been in Dublin; and I have been told, that the copy did not come over in the *Gazette*, but in the *London Journal*, or some other print of no authority or consequence. And, for anything that legally appears to the contrary, it may be a contrivance to fright us; or a project of some printer, who has a mind to make a penny by publishing something upon a subject which now employs all our thoughts in this kingdom. Mr. Wood, in publishing this paper, would insinuate to the world, as if the Committee had a greater concern for his credit, and private emolument, than for the honour of the Privy-council and both Houses of Parliament here, and for the quiet and welfare of this whole kingdom; for it seems intended as a vindication of Mr. Wood, not without several severe reflections on the Houses of Lords and Commons of Ireland. The whole is indeed written with the turn and air of a pamphlet; as if it were a dispute between William Wood on the one part, and the Lords Justices, Privy-council, and both Houses of Parliament, on the other; the design of it being to clear William Wood, and to charge the other side with casting rash and groundless aspersions upon him.

But, if it be really what the title imputes, Mr. Wood

has treated the Committee with great rudeness, by publishing an act of theirs in so unbecoming a manner, without their leave, and before it was communicated to the Government and Privy-council of Ireland, to whom the Committee advised that it should be transmitted.

But, with all deference be it spoken, I do not conceive that a Report of a Committee of the Council in England is hitherto a law in either kingdom; and, until any point is determined to be a law, it remains disputable by every subject. This, may it please your lords and worships, may seem a strange way of discoursing in an illiterate shopkeeper. I have endeavoured (although without the help of books) to improve that small portion of reason God has been pleased to give me; and when reason plainly appears before me, I cannot turn away my head from it. Thus, for instance, if any lawyer should tell me that such a point were law, from which many gross palpable absurdities must follow, I could not believe him. If Sir Edward Coke should positively assert (which he nowhere does, but the direct contrary) "that a limited prince could, by his prerogative, oblige his subjects to take half an ounce of lead, stamped with his image, for twenty shillings in gold," I should swear he was deceived, or a deceiver; because a power like that would leave the whole lives and fortunes of the people entirely at the mercy of the monarch ; yet this in effect is what Wood has advanced in some of his papers, and what suspicious people may possibly apprehend from some passages in what is called the Report.

That paper mentions such persons to have been examined, who were desirous and willing to be heard upon this subject. I am told they were four in all—Coleby, Brown, Mr. Finley the banker, and one more, whose name I know not. The first of these was tried for robbing the Treasury in Ireland ; and, though he was acquited for want of legal proof, yet every person in the Court believed him to be guilty.

The second stands recorded in the votes of the House of Commons, for endeavouring, by perjury and subornation, to take away the life of John Bingham, Esq.

But, since I have gone so far as to mention particular persons, it may be some satisfaction to know who is this Wood himself, that has the honour to have a whole kingdom at his mercy for almost two years together. I find he is in the patent entitled *esquire*, although he were understood to be only a hardware-man, and so I have been bold to call him in my former letters ; however a *'squire* he is, not only by virtue of his patent, but by having been a collector in Shropshire ; where, pretending to have been robbed, and suing the county, he was cast, and, for the infamy of the fact, lost his employment. I have heard another story of this 'Squire Wood, from a very honourable lady, that one Hamilton told her. Hamilton was sent for, six years ago, by Sir Isaac Newton, to try the coinage of four men, who then solicited a patent for coining halfpence for Ireland ; their names were Wood, Costor, Eliston, and Parker. Parker made the fairest offer, and Wood the worst ; for his coin was three halfpence in a pound weight less value than the other. By which it is plain, with what intentions he solicited his patent ; but not so plain how he obtained it.

It is alleged in the said paper, called the Report, " that upon repeated orders from a secretary of state, for sending over such papers and witnesses as should be thought proper to support the objections made against the patent by both Houses of Parliament, the Lord-Lieutenant represented the great difficulty he found himself in, to comply with these orders : that none of the principal members of both Houses, who were in the King's service or council, would take upon them to advise, how any material, person, or papers, might be sent over on this occasion," &c. And this is often re-peated, and represented as a proceeding that seems very extraordinary ; and that in a matter which had raised so great a clamour in Ireland, no person could be prevailed upon to come over from Ireland in support of the united sense of both Houses of Parliament in Ireland ; especially, that the chief difficulty should arise from a general apprehension of a miscarriage, in an inquiry before his Majesty, or in a proceeding by due course of law, in a case where both Houses of Parliament had declared themselves so fully convinced, and satisfied upon evidence and examinations taken in the most solemn manner.

How shall I, a poor ignorant shopkeeper, utterly unskilled in law, be able to answer so weighty an objection ? I will try what can be done by plain reason, unassisted by art, cunning, or eloquence.

In my humble opinion, the Committee of Council has already prejudged the whole case, by calling the united sense of both Houses of Parliament in Ireland "a universal clamour." Here the addresses of the Lords and Commons of Ireland, against a ruinous destructive project of an obscure single undertaker, is called "a clamour." I desire to know, how such a style would be resented in England from a Committee of Council there to a Parliament ; and how many impeachments would follow upon it ? But supposing the appellation to be proper, I never heard of a wise minister who despised the universal clamour of a people ; and if that clamour can be quieted by disappointing the fraudulent practice of a single person, the purchase is not exorbitant.

But, in answer to this objection ; first, it is manifest, that if this coinage had been in Ireland, with such limitations as have been formerly specified in other patents, and granted to persons of this kingdom, or even of England, able to give sufficient security, few or no inconveniences could have happened which might not have been immediately remedied. . . .

Put the case that the two Houses of Lords and Commons of England, and the Privy-council there should address his Majesty to recall a patent, from whence they apprehend the most ruinous consequences to the whole kingdom ; and to make it stronger, if possible, that the whole nation almost to a man, should thereupon discover "the most dismal apprehensions," as Mr. Wood styles them ; would his Majesty debate half an hour what he had to do ?

Would any minister dare to advise him against recalling such a patent ? Or would the matter be referred to the Privy-council, or to Westminster Hall ; the two Houses of Parliament plaintiffs, and William Wood defendant ? And is there even the smallest difference between the two cases ? Were not the people of Ireland

born as free as those of England? How have they forfeited their freedom? Is not their Parliament as fair a
representative of the people as that of England? And
has not their Privy-council as great, or a greater share
in the administration of public affairs? Are not they
subjects of the same King? Does not the same sun
shine upon them? And have they not the same God for
their protector? Am I a freeman in England, and do
I become a slave in six hours by crossing the Channel?
No wonder, then, if the boldest persons were cautious to
interpose in a matter already determined by the whole
voice of the nation, or to presume to represent the
representatives of the kingdom; and were justly appre-
hensive of meeting such a treatment as they would
deserve at the next session. It would seem very extraordinary, if any inferior court in England should take a
great matter out of the hands of the high court of Parliament during a prorogation, and decide it against the
opinion of both Houses. It happens so, however, that
although no persons were so bold as to go over as evidences, to prove the truth of the objections made against
this patent by the high court of Parliament here, yet
these objections stand good, notwithstanding the
answers made by Mr. Wood and his counsel.

The Report says, "That upon an assay made of the

fineness, weight, and value of this copper, it exceeded
in every article." This is possible enough in the pieces
on which the assay was made, but Wood must have
failed very much in point of dexterity, if he had not
taken care to provide a sufficient quantity of such halfpence as would bear the trial, which he was able to do,
although they were taken out of several parcels, since it
is now plain that the bias of favour has been wholly on
his side. . . .

As to what is alleged, that these halfpence far exceed
the like coinage for Ireland in the reigns of his Majesty's
predecessors, there cannot well be a more exceptional
way of arguing, although the fact were true; which,
however, is altogether mistaken, not by any fault in the
Committee, but by the fraud and imposition of Wood,
who certainly produced the worst patterns he could find;
such as were coined in small numbers by permissions to
private men, as butchers' halfpence, black dogs, and
others the like; or perhaps the small St. Patrick's coin
which passes now for a farthing, or at best some of the
smallest raps of the latest kind. For I have now by me
halfpence coined in the year 1680, by virtue of the
patent granted to my Lord Dartmouth, which was renewed to Knox, and they are heavier by a ninth part
than those of Wood, and of much better metal, and

F

the great St. Patrick's halfpence are yet larger than either.

But what is all this to the present debate ?

If, under the various exigencies of former times, by wars, rebellions, and insurrections, the Kings of England were sometimes forced to pay their armies here with mixed or base money, God forbid that the necessities of turbulent times should be a precedent for times of peace, and order, and settlement.

In the patent above-mentioned, granted to Lord Dartmouth in the reign of King Charles II., and renewed to Knox, the securities given into the exchequer, obliging the patentee to receive his money back upon every demand, were an effectual remedy against all inconveniences, and the copper was coined in our own kingdom ; so that we were in no danger to purchase it with the loss of all our silver and gold carried over to another, nor to be at the trouble of going to England for the redressing of any abuse. . . .

Among other clauses mentioned in this patent, to show how advantageous it is to Ireland, there is one which seems to be of a singular nature : " That the patentee shall be obliged, during his term, to pay eight hundred pounds a year to the Crown, and two hundred pounds a year to the comptroller." I have heard,

indeed, that the King's council do always consider, in
the passing of a patent, whether it will be of advantage
to the Crown ; but I have likewise heard, that it is at the
same time considered whether passing of it may be in-
jurious to any other persons or bodies politic. However, although the attorney and solicitor be servants to
the King, and therefore bound to consult his Majesty's
interest, yet I am under some doubt whether eight
hundred pounds a year to the Crown would be equivalent
to the ruin of a kingdom. It would be far better for
us to have paid eight thousand pounds a-year into his
Majesty's coffers, in the midst of all our taxes (which,
in proportion, are greater in this kingdom than ever
they were in England, even during the war), than purchase such an addition to the revenue at the price of our
utter undoing. But here it is plain that fourteen
thousand pounds are to be paid by Wood, only as a
small circumstantial charge for the purchase of his
patent. What were his other visible costs I know not,
and what were his latent is variously conjectured, but he
must surely be a man of some wonderful merit. Has
he saved any other kingdom at his own expense, to give
him a title of reimbursing himself by the destruction of
ours ? Has he discovered the longitude or the universal
medicine ? No ; but he has found the philosopher's

stone after a new manner, by debasing copper, and resolving to force it upon us for gold.

When the two Houses represented to his Majesty that the patent to Wood was obtained in a clandestine manner, surely the Committee could not think the Parliament would insinuate, that it had not passed in the common forms, and run through every office where fees and perquisites were due. They knew very well, that persons in places were no enemies to grants ; and that the officers of the Crown could not be kept in the dark. But the late Lord-Lieutenant of Ireland[7] affirmed it was a secret to him ; and who will doubt his veracity, especially when he swore to a person of quality, from whom I had it, "that Ireland should never be troubled with these halfpence" ? It was a secret to the people of Ireland, who were to be the only sufferers ; and those who but knew the state of the kingdom, and were most able to advise in such an affair, were wholly strangers to it.

It is allowed by the Report, that this patent was passed without the knowledge of the chief governor or officers of Ireland ; and it is there elaborately shown, that former patents have passed in the same manner, and are good in law. I shall not dispute legality of

[7] The Duke of Grafton.

patents, but am ready to suppose it in his Majesty's power to grant a patent for stamping round bits of copper to every subject he has.

Therefore, to lay aside the point of law, I would only put the question, whether, in reason and justice, it would not have been proper, in an affair upon which the welfare of this depends, that the said King should have received timely notice ; and the matter not be carried on between the patentee, and the officers of the Crown, who were to be the only gainers by it. . . .

But suppose there were not one single halfpenny of copper coin in this whole kingdom (which Mr. Wood seems to intend, unless we will come to his terms, as appears by employing his emissaries to buy up our old ones at a penny in the shilling more than they pass for), it could not be any real evil to us, although it might be some inconvenience. We have many sorts of small silver coins, to which they are strangers in England ; such as the French threepences, fourpence-halfpennies, and eightpence-farthings, the Scotch fivepences and tenpences, besides their twenty-pences and three-and-four-pences, by which we are able to make change to a halfpenny of almost any piece of gold and silver ; and if we are driven to the expedient of a sealed card, with the little gold and silver still remaining, it will, I suppose, be somewhat better, than to have nothing left, but Wood's adulterated copper, which he is neither obliged by his patent, nor HITHERTO able by his estate, to make good. . . .

The sum of the whole is this. The Committee advises the King to send immediate orders to all his officers here, that Wood's coin be suffered and permitted, without any let, suit, trouble, &c., to pass and be received as current money, by such as shall be willing to receive the same. It is probable that the first willing receivers may be those who must receive it whether they will or not, at least under the penalty of losing an office. But the landed undepending men, the merchants, the shopkeepers, and bulk of the people, I hope and am almost confident, will never receive it. What must the consequence be? The owners will sell it for as much as they can get.

Wood's halfpence will come to be offered for six a penny (yet then he will be a sufficient gainer), and the necessary receivers will be losers of two-thirds in their salaries or pay.

I am very sensible that such a work as I have undertaken might have worthily employed a much better pen ; but when a house is attempted to be robbed, it often happens the weakest in the family runs first to the door.

All the assistance I had were some informations from an eminent person; whereof I am afraid I have spoiled a few, by endeavouring to make them of a piece with my own productions, and the rest I was not able to manage. I was in the case of David, who could not move in the armour of Saul; and therefore I chose to attack this uncircumcised Philistine (Wood, I mean) with a sling and a stone. And I may say, for Wood's honour, as well as my own, that he resembles Goliah in many circumstances very applicable to the present purpose; for Goliah had "a helmet of brass upon his head, and he was armed with a coat of mail; and the weight of the coat was five thousand shekels of brass; and he had greaves of brass upon his legs, and a target of brass between his shoulders."

In short, he was like Mr. Wood, all over brass, and he defied the armies of the living God. Goliah's conditions of combat were likewise the same with those of Wood's, "If he prevail against us, then shall we be his servants." But if it happens that I prevail over him, I renounce the other part of the condition: "He shall never be a servant of mine; for I do not think him fit to be trusted in any honest man's shop."

FOURTH LETTER.

IRELAND is here summoned to assert her independence in the indignant voice of a nation that has borne the yoke of slavery far too long. Every line in this letter is instinct with life, and thrilling with sarcastic force. No more waste of words. The question is simply one of might against right: as old as human nature, but never brought into shorter compass. The printer of this letter was thrown into prison, as if to shame the undoubted author into surrender. Ireland was now under a new rule, the refined and cultivated Carteret was appointed Lord-Lieutenant in 1724. Swift used the privilege of an old friend in writing to him freely on the subject of the coinage. He was sorry to see his friend used as the tool of the Government, which occasioned the outburst, "What in God's name do *you* here? Get you gone, and send us our boobies again."

LETTER IV.

To the whole People of Ireland.

October 23rd, 1724.

MY DEAR COUNTRYMEN,

Having already written three letters upon so disagreeable a subject as Mr. Wood and his halfpence, I conceived my task was at an end; but I find that cordials must be frequently applied to weak constitutions, political as well as natural. A people long used to hardships lose by degrees the very notions of liberty. They look upon themselves as creatures at mercy, and that all impositions, laid on them by a stronger hand, are, in the phrase of the Report, legal and obligatory. Hence proceed that poverty and lowness of spirit, to which a kingdom may be subject, as well as a particular person. And when Esau came fainting from the field at the point to die, it is no wonder that he sold his birthright for a mess of pottage. I thought I had sufficiently shown, to all who could want instruction, by what methods they might safely proceed, wherever this coin should be offered to them; and, I believe, there has not been, for many ages, an example of any kingdom so firmly united in a point of great importance, as this of ours is at present against that detestable fraud. But, however, it so happens, that some weak people begin to be alarmed anew by rumours industriously spread. Wood prescribes to the newsmongers in London what they are to write. In one of their papers, published here by some obscure printer, and certainly with a bad design, we are told, " That the Papists in Ireland have entered into an association against his coin," although it be notoriously known, that they never once offered to stir in the matter; so that the two Houses of Parliament, the Privy-council, the great number of corporations, the Lord Mayor and aldermen of Dublin, the grand juries, and principal gentlemen of several counties, are stigmatized in a lump under the name of "Papists." This impostor and his crew do likewise give out, that, by refusing to receive his dross for sterling, we "dispute the King's prerogative, are grown ripe for rebellion, and ready to shake off the dependency of Ireland upon the crown of England."

To countenance which reports, he has published a paragraph in another newspaper, to let us know, that "the Lord-Lieutenant is ordered to come over immediately to settle his halfpence."

I entreat you, my dear countrymen, not to be under the least concern upon these and the like rumours, which are no more than the last howls of a dog dissected alive, as I hope he has sufficiently been. These calumnies are the only reserve that is left him. For surely our continued and (almost) unexampled loyalty, will never be called in question, for not suffering ourselves to be robbed of all that we have by one obscure ironmonger.

As to disputing the King's prerogative, give me leave to explain, to those who are ignorant, what the meaning of that word *prerogative* is.

The Kings of these realms enjoy several powers, wherein the laws have not interposed. So, they can make war and peace without the consent of Parliament—and this is a very great prerogative; but if the Parliament does not approve of the war, the King must bear the charge of it out of his own purse—and this is ·a great check on the crown.

So, the King has a prerogative to coin money without consent of Parliament; but he cannot compel the subject to take that money, except it be sterling gold or silver, because herein he is limited by law. Some princes have, indeed, extended their prerogative farther than the law allowed them; wherein, however, the lawyers of succeeding ages, as fond as they are of precedents, have never dared to justify them. But, to say the truth, it is only of late times that prerogative has been fixed and ascertained; for, whoever reads the history of England will find, that some former Kings, and those none of the worst, have, upon several occasions, ventured to control the laws, with very little ceremony or scruple, even later than the days of Queen Elizabeth. In her reign, that pernicious counsel of sending base money hither, very narrowly failed of losing the kingdom—being complained of by the lord-deputy, the council, and the whole body of the English here; so that, soon after her death, it

was recalled by her successor, and lawful money paid
in exchange.

Having thus given you some notion of what is meant
by " the King's prerogative," as far as a tradesman can
be thought capable of explaining it, I will only add the
opinion of the great Lord Bacon : " That, as God governs
the world by the settled laws of nature, which He has
made, and never transcends those laws but upon high
important occasions, so among earthly princes, those
are the wisest and the best, who govern by the known
laws of the country, and seldomest make use of their
prerogative."

Now here you may see, that the vile accusation of
Wood and his accomplices, charging us with disputing
the King's prerogative by refusing his brass, can have
no place—because compelling the subject to take any
coin which is not sterling, is no part of the King's
prerogative, and I am very confident, if it were so, we
should be the last of his people to dispute it ; as well
from that inviolable loyalty we have always paid to his
Majesty, as from the treatment we might, in such a case,
justly expect from some, who seem to think we have
neither common sense nor common senses. But, God
be thanked, the best of them are only our fellow-subjects,
and not our masters. One great merit I am sure we

have, which those of English birth can have no pretence to—that our ancestors reduced this kingdom to the obedience of England ; for which we have been rewarded with a worse climate—the privilege of being governed by laws to which we do not consent—a ruined trade— a House of Peers without jurisdiction—almost an incapacity for all employments—and the dread of Wood's halfpence.

But we are so far from disputing the King's prerogative in coining, that we own he has power to give a patent to any man for selling his royal image and superscription upon whatever materials he pleases, and liberty to the patentee to offer them in any country from England to Japan ; only attended with one small limitation—that nobody alive is obliged to take them. . . .

Let me now say something concerning the other great cause of some people's fear, as Wood has taught the London newswriter to express it, that his excellency the Lord-Lieutenant is coming over to settle Wood's halfpence. We know very well, that the Lord-Lieutenants for several years past, have not thought this kingdom worthy the honour of their residence longer than was absolutely necessary for the King's business, which, consequently, wanted no speed in the

despatch. And therefore it naturally fell into most
men's thoughts, that a new governor, coming at an
unusual time, must portend some unusual business to
be done; especially if the common report be true,
that the Parliament, prorogued to I know not when,
is, by a new summons, revoking that prorogation, to
assemble soon after the arrival; for which extraordinary proceeding, the lawyers on the other side
the water have, by great good fortune, found two
precedents.

All this being granted, it can never enter into my
head, that so little a creature as Wood could find
credit enough with the King and his ministers, to
have the Lord-Lieutenant of Ireland sent hither in a
hurry upon his errand.

For, let us take the whole matter nakedly as it lies
before us, without the refinements of some people,
with which we have nothing to do.

Here is a patent granted under the great seal of
England, upon false suggestions, to one William Wood
for coining copper halfpence for Ireland. The Parliament here, upon apprehensions of the worst consequences from the said patent, address the King to
have it recalled. This is refused; and a Committee
of the Privy-council report to his Majesty, that Wood

has performed the conditions of his patent. He then is left to do the best he can with his halfpence, no man being obliged to receive them ; the people here, being likewise left to themselves, unite as one man, resolving they will have nothing to do with his ware.

By this plain account of the fact it is manifest, that the King and his ministry are wholly out of the case, and the matter is left to be disputed between him and us. Will any man, therefore, attempt to persuade me, that a Lord-Lieutenant is to be despatched over in great haste before the ordinary time, and a Parliament summoned by anticipating a prorogation, merely to put a hundred thousand pounds into the pocket of a sharper by the ruin of a most loyal kingdom?

But, supposing all this to be true, by what arguments could a Lord-Lieutenant prevail on the same Parliament, which addressed with so much zeal and earnestness against this evil, to pass it into a law ? I am sure their opinion of Wood and his project is not mended since their last prorogation; and, supposing those methods should be used, which detractors tell us have been sometimes put in practice for gaining votes, it is well known, that, in this kingdom, there are few employments to be given ; and, if there were more, it is as well known to whose share they must fall. But, because great numbers of you are altogether ignorant of the affairs of your country, I will tell you some reasons why there are so few employments to be disposed of in this kingdom. All considerable offices for life are here possessed by those to whom the reversions were granted ; and these have been generally followers of the chief governors, or persons who had interest in the Court of England. So, the Lord Berkeley of Stratton holds that great office of Master of the rolls ; the Lord Palmerstown is first re-membrancer, worth near 2000l. per annum. One Dod-dington, secretary to the Earl of Pembroke, begged the reversion of clerk of the pells, worth 2500l. a-year, which he now enjoys by the death of the Lord Newtown. Mr. Southwell is secretary of State, and the Earl of Bur-lington lord high treasurer of Ireland by inheritance. These are only a few among many others which I have been told of, but cannot remember. Nay, the reversion of several employments, during pleasure, is granted the same way. This, among many others, is a circumstance, whereby the kingdom of Ireland is distinguished from all other nations upon earth ; and makes it so difficult an affair to get into a civil employ, that Mr. Addison was forced to purchase an old obscure place, called keeper of the records in Bermingham's Tower, of 10l. a-year, and to get a salary of 400l. annexed to it, though all the records there are not worth half-a-crown, either for curiosity or use. And we lately saw a favourite secretary descend to be master of the revels,[8] which, by his credit and extortion, he has made pretty considerable. I say nothing of the under-treasurership, worth about 9000*l*. a year, nor of the commissioners of the revenue, four of whom generally live in England, for I think none of these are granted in reversion ; but the jest is, that I have known, upon occasion, some of these absent officers as keen against the interest of Ireland, as if they had never been indebted to her for a single groat.

I confess, I have been sometimes tempted to wish that this project of Wood's might succeed ; because I reflected with some pleasure, what a jolly crew it would bring over among us of lords and squires, and pensioners of both sexes, and officers civil and military, where we should live together as merry and sociable as beggars, only with this one abatement, that we should neither have meat to feed, nor manufactures to clothe us, unless we could be content to prance about in coats of mail, or eat brass as ostriches do iron.

I return from this digression to that which gave me the occasion of making it. And I believe you are now

[8] Mr. Hopkins, the Duke of Grafton's secretary.

convinced, that if the Parliament of Ireland were as
temptable as any other assembly within a mile of Chris-
tendom (which God forbid !), yet the managers must of
necessity fail for want of tools to work with.   But I will
yet go one step farther, by supposing that a hundred
new employments were erected on purpose to gratify
compliers, yet still an insuperable difficulty would remain.
For it happens, I know not how, that money is neither
Whig nor Tory—neither of town nor country party, and
it is not improbable that a gentleman would rather
choose to live upon his own estate, which brings
him gold and silver, than with the addition of an
employment, when his rents and salary must both
be paid in Wood's brass, at above eighty per cent.
discount.

For these, and many other reasons, I am confident
you need not be under the least apprehension from the
sudden expectation of the Lord-Lieutenant,[9] while we
continue in our present hearty disposition, to alter which
no suitable temptation can possibly be offered.   And if,
as I have often asserted from the best authority, the law
has not left a power in the crown to force any money,

[9] Lord Carteret, afterwards Earl Granville. As the ally of
Bolingbroke, and opponent of Walpole, he was to some extent a
favourite of Swift.

except sterling, upon the subject, much less can the crown devolve such a power upon another. . . .

Another slander spread by Wood and his emissaries is, "That by opposing him we discover an inclination to throw off our dependence upon the crown of England." Pray observe how important a person is this same William Wood, and how the public weal of two kingdoms is involved in his private interest. First, all those who refuse to take his coin are Papists; for he tells us, "That none but Papists are associated against him." Secondly, "they dispute the King's prerogative." Thirdly, "they are ripe for rebellion." And, fourthly "they are going to shake off their dependence upon the crown of England;" that is to say, they are going to choose another king, for there can be no other meaning in this expression, however some may pretend to strain it.

And this gives me an opportunity of explaining to those who are ignorant, another point, which has often swelled in my breast. Those who come over hither to us from England, and some weak people among ourselves, whenever in discourse we make mention of liberty and property, shake their heads, and tell us that Ireland is a depending kingdom; as if they would seem by this phrase to intend that the people of Ireland are in some state of slavery or dependence different from those of England ; whereas a depending kingdom is a modern term of art, unknown, as I have heard, to all ancient civilians, and writers upon government ; and Ireland is, on the contrary, called in some statutes "an imperial crown," as held only from God, which is as high a style as any kingdom is capable of receiving. Therefore, by this expression, "a depending kingdom," there is no more to be understood than that, by a statute made here in the thirty-third year of Henry VIII., the King and his successors are to be kings imperial of this realm, as united and knit to the imperial crown of England. I have looked over all the English and Irish statutes, without finding any law that makes Ireland depend upon England, any more than England does upon Ireland. We have, indeed, obliged ourselves to have the same King with them, and consequently they are obliged to have the same King with us. For the law was made by our own Parliament, and our ancestors then were not such fools (whatever they were in the preceding reign) to bring themselves under I know not what dependence, which is now talked of, without any ground of law, reason, or common sense. Let whoever thinks other-wise, I, M. B., Drapier, desire to be excepted ; for I declare, next under God, I depend only on the King my

sovereign, and on the laws of my own country. And I
am so far from depending on the people of England,
that if ever they should rebel against my sovereign
(which God forbid !) I would be ready, at the first command from his Majesty, to take arms against them, as
some of my countrymen did against theirs at Preston.
And if such a rebellion should prove so successful as to
fix the Pretender on the throne of England, I would
venture to transgress that statute so far as to lose every
drop of my blood to hinder him from being King of
Ireland.

It is true, indeed, that within the memory of man,
the Parliaments of England have sometimes assumed
the power of binding this kingdom by laws enacted
there ;[1] wherein they were at first openly opposed (as
far as truth, reason and justice,[2] are capable of opposing)
by the famous Mr. Molineux, an English gentleman
born here, as well as by several of the greatest patriots
and best Whigs in England ; but the love and torrent
of power prevailed. Indeed the arguments on both

---

[1] This was especially the case in the reign of William III., when
the doctrine of English supremacy was assumed in order to dis-
credit the authority of the Irish Parliament summoned by James II.

[2] William Molineux, the friend of Locke, who wrote a pamphlet,
published in 1698, against the oppressive laws adopted by England
in regard to Irish Manufactures.

sides were invincible. For, in reason, all government without the consent of the governed, is the very definition of slavery ; but, in fact, eleven men well armed will certainly subdue one single man in his shirt. But I have done ; for those who have used to cramp liberty, have gone so far as to resent even the liberty of complaining ; although a man upon the rack was never known to be refused the liberty of roaring as loud as he thought fit.

And as we are apt to sink too much under unreasonable fears, so we are too soon inclined to be raised by groundless hopes, according to the nature of all consumptive bodies like ours. Thus it has been given about, for several days past, that somebody in England empowered a second somebody, to write to a third somebody here, to assure us that we should no more be troubled with these halfpence. And this is reported to have been done by the same person, who is said to have sworn some months ago, " that he would ram them down our throats," though I doubt they would stick in our stomachs ; but whichever of these reports be true or false, it is no concern of ours. For, in this point, we have nothing to do with English ministers ; and I should be sorry to leave it in their power to redress this grievance, or to enforce it; for the report of the Committee has given me a surfeit.

The remedy is wholly in your own hands; and therefore I have digressed a little, in order to refresh and continue that spirit so seasonably raised among you; and to let you see, that by the laws of GOD, of NATURE, of NATIONS, and of your COUNTRY, you ARE, and OUGHT to be, as FREE a people as your brethren in England. . . .

THE FIFTH LETTER

WAS addressed to Viscount Molesworth, a distinguished Whig; and the author of several works written in a patriotic spirit. His agricultural treatise on Ireland was highly approved by Swift. This closed the series for the present. The tone of the letter is apologetic. Hitherto he has not shaken off the impression left by the works of Lord Molesworth himself, of Locke, of Molyneux and Sidney, who talked of liberty as a common blessing. But now he will "grow wiser and learn to consider my driver, the road I am in, and with whom I am yoked."

LETTER V.

To the Right Honourable the Lord Viscount Molesworth.

DIRECTIONS TO THE PRINTER.

From my shop in St. Francis' Street,

December 24th, 1724.

MR. HARDING,

When I sent you my former papers, I cannot
say I intended you either good or hurt ; and yet you
have happened, through my means, to receive both.   I
pray God deliver you from any more of the latter, and
increase the former.   Your trade, particularly in this
kingdom, is, of all others, the most unfortunately
circumstantiated ; for as you deal in the most worthless
kind of trash, the penny productions of pennyless
scribblers, so you often venture your liberty, and
sometimes your lives, for the purchase of half-a-crown ;
and, by your own ignorance, are punished for other
men's actions.   I am afraid, you, in particular, think
you have reason to complain of me, for your own and
your wife's confinement in prison, to your great expense
as well as hardship, and for a prosecution still im-
pending.   But I will tell you, Mr. Harding, how that
matter stands.

Since the press has lain under so strict an inspection, those who have a mind to inform the world are become so cautious, as to keep themselves, if possible, out of the way of danger. My custom, therefore, is, to dictate to a 'prentice,[3] who can write in a feigned hand, and what is written we send to your house by a blackguard boy. But at the same time I do assure you, upon my reputation, that I never did send you anything for which I thought you could possibly be called to an account ; and you will be my witness, that I always desired you, by letter, to take some good advice, before you ventured to print, because I knew the dexterity of dealers in the law at finding out something to fasten on, where no evil is meant. I am told, indeed, that you did accordingly consult several very able persons, and even some who afterwards appeared against you ; to which I can only answer, that you must either change your advisers, or determine to print nothing that comes from a Drapier.

I desire you to send the enclosed letter, directed, " To my Lord Viscount Molesworth, at his house at Brackdenstown, near Swords ;" but I would have it sent printed, for the convenience of his Lordship's reading,

[3] There was a certain amount of truth in this. The Dean's butler acted as amanuensis.

because this counterfeit hand of my apprentice is not very legible. And, if you think fit to publish it, I would have you first get it read over by some notable lawyer. I am assured, you will find enough of them who are friends to the Drapier, and will do it without a fee; which, I am afraid, you can ill-afford after all your expenses. For although I have taken so much care, that I think it impossible to find a topic out of the following papers for sending you again to prison, yet I will not venture to be your guarantee.

This ensuing letter contains only a short account of myself, and an humble apology for my former pamphlets, especially the last, with little mention of Mr. Wood for his halfpence, because I have already said enough upon that subject, until occasion shall be given for new fears; and, in that case, you may perhaps hear from me again.

I am your friend and servant,

M. B.

P.S.—For want of intercourse between you and me, which I never will suffer, your people are apt to make very gross errors in the press, which I desire you will provide against.

A LETTER

*To the Right Honourable the Lord Viscount Molesworth,
at his house at Brackdenstown, near Swords.*

From my shop in St. Francis Street,
December 14*th,* 1724.

MY LORD,

I reflect too late on the maxim of common observers, "that those who meddle in matters out of their calling will have reason to repent;" which is now verified in me: for, by engaging in the trade of a writer, I have drawn upon myself the displeasure of the government, signified by a proclamation, promising a reward of three hundred pounds to the first faithful subject who shall be able and inclined to inform against me; to which I may add the laudable zeal and industry of my Lord Chief Justice Whitshed, in his endeavours to discover so dangerous a person. Therefore, whether I repent or not, I have certainly cause to do so; and the common observation still stands good.

It will sometimes happen, I know not how, in the course of human affairs, that a man shall be made liable to legal animadversion where he has nothing to answer for either to God or his country, and condemned at

Westminster Hall for what he will never be charged with at the day of judgment.

After strictly examining my own heart, and consulting some divines of great reputation, I cannot accuse myself of any malice or wickedness against the public, —of any designs to sow sedition,—of reflecting on the King and his ministers,—or of endeavouring to alienate the affections of the people of this kingdom from those of England.[4] All I can charge myself with is, a weak attempt to serve a nation in danger of destruction by a most wicked and malicious projector, without waiting until I were called to its assistance ; which attempt, however it may perhaps give me the title of *pragmatical* and *overweening*, will never lie a burden upon my conscience.

God knows, whether I may not, with all my caution, have already run myself into a second danger by offering thus much in my own vindication ; for I have heard of a judge, who, upon the criminal's appeal to the dreadful day of judgment, told him he had incurred a *premunire*, for appealing to a foreign jurisdiction ; and of another in Wales, who severely checked the prisoner for offering the same plea, taxing him with " reflecting on the Court

---

[4] Articles mentioned in the indictment and proclamation.

by such a comparison, because comparisons were odious."

But, in order to make some excuse for being more speculative than others of my condition, I desire your Lordship's pardon, while I am doing a very foolish thing; which is, to give you some little account of myself.

I was bred at a free school, where I acquired some little knowledge in the Latin tongue. I served my apprenticeship in London, and there set up for myself with good success ; until, by the death of some friends, and the misfortunes of others, I returned into this kingdom, and began to employ my thoughts in cultivating the woollen manufacture through all its branches, where-in I met with great discouragement and powerful opposers, whose objections appeared to me very strange and singular. They argued, "that the people of England would be offended if our manufactures were brought to equal theirs ; " and even some of the weaving trade were my enemies, which I could not but look upon as absurd and unnatural. I remember your lordship, at that time, did me the honour to come into my shop, where I showed you a piece of black and white stuff just sent from the dyer,[5] which you were pleased to approve of, and be my customer for.

[5] His " Proposal for the Universal Use of Irish Manufactures."

However, I was so mortified, that I resolved, for the future, to sit quietly in my shop, and deal in common goods, like the rest of my brethren ; until it happened, some months ago, considering with myself that the lower and poorer sort of people wanted a plain, strong, coarse stuff, to defend them against cold easterly winds, which then blew very fierce and blasting for a long time together, I contrived one[6] on purpose, which sold very well all over the kingdom, and preserved many thousands from agues.   I then made a second and a third kind of stuffs[7] for the gentry with the same success ; insomuch, that an ague has hardly been heard of for some time.

This incited me so far, that I ventured upon a fourth piece,[8] made of the best Irish wool I could get ; and I thought it grave and rich enough to be worn by the best lord or judge of the land.   But of late some great folks complain, as I hear, " that, when they had it on, they felt a shuddering in their limbs,"—and have thrown it off in a rage, cursing to hell the poor Drapier who invented it ; so that I am determined never to work for persons of quality again, except for your lordship, and a very few more.

6   The first " Letter."
7   The second and third " Letters."
8   The fourth " Letter," the cause of the indictment and proclamation.

I assure your lordship, upon the word of an honest citizen, that I am not richer, by the value of one of Mr. Wood's halfpence, with the sale of all the several stuffs I have contrived, for I give the whole profit to the dyers and pressers; [9] and, therefore, I hope you will please to believe, that no other motive, beside the love of my country, could engage me to busy my head and hands, to the loss of my time, and the gain of nothing but vexation and ill-will.

I have now in hand one piece of stuff, to be woven on purpose for your lordship; although I might be ashamed to offer it to you after I have confessed, that it will be made only from the shreds and remnants of the wool employed in the former. However, I shall work it up as well as I can; and, at worst, you need only give it among your tenants. . . .

I am told that the two points in my last letter, from which an occasion of offence has been taken, are where I mention his Majesty's answer to the address of the House of Lords upon Mr. Wood's patent; and where I discourse upon Ireland's being a dependent kingdom. As to the former, I can only say that I have treated it with the utmost respect and caution; and I thought it necessary to show where Wood's patent differed, in many

[9] Printers.

essential parts, from all others that ever had been granted;
because the contrary had, for want of due information,
been so strongly and so largely asserted. As to the
other, of Ireland's dependency, I confess to have often
heard it mentioned, but was never able to understand
what it meant. This gave me the curiosity to inquire
among several eminent lawyers, who professed they
knew nothing of the matter. I then turned over all the
statutes of both kingdoms, without the least information,
farther than an Irish act, that I quoted, of the 33rd of
Henry VIII., uniting Ireland to England under one
King. I cannot say I was sorry to be disappointed in
my search, because it is certain I could be contented to
depend only upon God and my prince, and the laws of
my own country, after the manner of other nations.
But since my betters are of a different opinion, and desire
farther dependencies, I shall outwardly submit; yet still
insisting in my own heart, upon the exception I made
of M. B., Drapier. . . . All I desire is, that the cause of
my country against Mr. Wood, may not suffer by any
inadvertency of mine. Whether Ireland depends upon
England or only upon God, the King, and the law, I
hope no man will assert that it depends upon Mr. Wood.
I should be heartily sorry that this commendable spirit
against me should accidentally (and what, I hope, was

never intended) strike a damp upon that spirit in all
ranks and corporations of men against the desperate and
ruinous design of Mr. Wood. Let my countrymen blot
out those parts in my last letter which they dislike ; and
let no rust remain on my sword, to cure the wounds
I have given to our most mortal enemy. When Sir
Charles Sedley was taking the oaths, where several
things were to be renounced, he said, " he loved renouncing ; " asked, " if any more were to be renounced ; for he
was ready to renounce as much as they pleased."
Although I am not so thorough a renouncer, yet let me
have but good city-security against this pestilent coinage,
and I shall be ready not only to renounce every syllable
in all my four letters, but to deliver them cheerfully with
my own hands into those of the common hangman, to
be burnt with no better company than the coiner's
effigies, if any part of it has escaped out of the secular
hands of my faithful friends, the common people. But,
whatever the sentiments of some people may be, I think
it is agreed that many of those who subscribed against
me, are on the side of a vast majority in the kingdom
who opposed Mr. Wood ; and it was with great satisfaction that I observed some right honourable names
very amicably joined with my own, at the bottom of a
strong declaration against him and his coin. But if the

admission of it among us be already determined, the
worthy person who is to betray me ought in prudence
to do it with all convenient speed ; or else it may be
difficult to find three hundred pounds sterling for the
discharge of his hire, when the public shall have lost
five hundred thousand, if there be so much in the nation ;
besides four-fifths of its annual income for ever.   I
am told by lawyers, that in quarrels between man and
man, it is of much weight which of them gave the first
provocation, or struck the first blow.   It is manifest that
Mr. Wood has done both, and therefore I should humbly
propose to have him first hanged, and his dross thrown
into the sea ; after which the Drapier will be ready to
stand his trial.   " It must needs be that offences come,
but woe unto him by whom the offence comes."
If Mr. Wood had held his hand, everybody else would
have held their tongues ; and then there would have
been little need of pamphlets, juries, or proclamations,
upon this occasion.   The provocation must needs have
been very great, which could stir up an obscure, indolent
Drapier, to become an author.   One would almost think,
the very stones in the street would rise up in such a
cause ; and I am not sure they will not do so against
Mr. Wood, if ever he comes within their reach.   It is a
known story of the dumb boy, whose tongue forced a

passage for speech by the horror of seeing a dagger at his father's throat. This may lessen the wonder, that a tradesman, hid in privacy and silence should cry out when the life and being of his political mother are attempted before his face, and by so infamous a wretch.

I am now resolved to follow (after the usual proceeding of mankind, because it is too late) the advice given, me by a certain Dean.[1] He showed the mistake I was in of trusting to the general good-will of the people ; that I had succeeded hitherto better than could be expected ; but that some unfortunate circumstantial lapse would bring me within the reach of power ; that my good intentions would be no security against those who watched every motion of my pen in the bitterness of my soul." He produced an instance of "a writer as innocent, as disinterested, and as well-meaning as myself ; who had written a very seasonable and inoffensive treatise, exhorting the people of this kingdom to wear their own manufactures ;[2] for which, however, the printer, was prosecuted with the utmost virulence ; the jury sent back nine times ; and the man given up to the mercy of the Court." The Dean farther observed, "that

---

[1] He probably speaks of himself.
[2] The " Proposal for the Use of Irish Manufactures."

I was in a manner left alone to stand the battle; while others, who had ten thousand times better talents than a Drapier, were so prudent as to lie still; and perhaps thought it no unpleasant amusement to look on with safety, while another was giving them diversion at the hazard of his liberty and fortune; and thought they made a sufficient recompense by a little applause." Whereupon he concluded with a short story of a Jew at Madrid, who, being condemned to the fire on account of his religion, a crowd of schoolboys following him to the stake, and apprehending they might lose their sport if he should happen to recant, would often clap him on the back, and cry, " *Sta firme, Moyse:* Moses, continue steadfast."

I allow this gentleman's advice to have been very good, and his observations just; and in one respect my condition is worse than that of the Jew; for no re-cantation will save me. However, it should seem, by some late proceedings, that my state is not altogether deplorable. This I can impute to nothing but the steadiness of two impartial grand juries; which has confirmed in me an opinion I have long entertained; that, as philosophers say, virtue is seated in the middle; so, in another sense, the little virtue left in the world, is chiefly to be found among the middle rank of mankind.

who are neither allured out of her paths by ambition,
nor driven by poverty. . . .

But, to confess the truth, my lord, I begin to grow
weary of my office as a writer, and could heartily wish
it were devolved upon my brethren, the makers of songs
and ballads, who perhaps are the best qualified at present
to gather up the gleanings of this controversy. As to
myself, it has been my misfortune to begin and pursue
it upon a wrong foundation. For, having detected the
frauds and falsehoods of this vile impostor Wood in
every part, I foolishly disdained to have recourse to
whining, lamenting, and crying for mercy; but rather
chose to appeal to law and liberty, and the common
rights of mankind, without considering the climate I
was in. Since your last residence in Ireland, I frequently
have taken my nag to ride about your grounds, where
I fancied myself to feel an air of freedom breathing
around me; and I am glad the low condition of a tradesman did not qualify me to wait on you at your house;
for then I am afraid my writings would not have
escaped severer censures. But I have lately sold my
nag, and honestly told his greatest fault, which was
that of snuffing up the air about Brackdenstown;
whereby he became such a lover of liberty, that I could
scarce hold him in. I have likewise buried, at the

bottom of a strong chest, your lordship's writings, under a heap of others that treat of liberty, and spread over a layer or two of Hobbes, Filmer, Bodin, and many more authors of that stamp, to be readiest at hand whenever I shall be disposed to take up a new set of principles in government. In the meantime, I design quietly to look to my shop, and keep as far out of your lordship's influence as possible ; and if you ever see any more of my writings on this subject, I promise you shall find them as innocent, as insipid, and without a sting, as what I have now offered you. But, if your lordship will please to give me an easy lease of some part of your estate in Yorkshire, thither will I carry my chest, and, turning it upside down, resume my political reading where I left off, feed on plain homely fare, and live and die a free, honest English farmer ; but not without regret for leaving my countrymen under the dread of the brazen talons of Mr. Wood ;—my most loyal and innocent countrymen, to whom I owe so much for their good opinion of me, and my poor endeavours to serve them.

I am, with the greatest respect,

My Lord,

Your Lordship's most obedient, and most humble servant,

M. B.

SIXTH LETTER

WAS written a little after the proclamation against the Drapier's fourth Letter. It is delivered with much caution, because the Author confesses himself to be the Dean of St. Patrick's.

LETTER VI.

To the Lord Chancellor Middleton.

Deanery-house, *October*, 1724.

MY LORD,

I desire you will consider me as a member who comes in at the latter end of a debate ; or as a lawyer who speaks to a cause when the matter has been almost exhausted by those who spoke before.

I remember, some months ago, I was at your house upon a commission, where I am one of the governors ; but I went thither, not so much on account of the commission, as to ask you some questions concerning Mr. Wood's patent to coin halfpence for Ireland ; where you very freely told me, in a mixed company, how much you had always been against that wicked project ;[3] which

---

[3] Though he signed the proclamation against the author of the Drapier's Letters, Lord Middleton was himself inimical to Wood's project.

raised in me an esteem for you so far that I went in a few days to make you a visit, after many years' intermission. I am likewise told that your son wrote two letters from London (one of which I have seen), empowering those to whom they were directed to assure his friends, that whereas there was a malicious report spread of his engaging himself to Mr. Walpole for forty thousand pounds of Wood's coin to be received in Ireland, the said report was false and groundless; and he had never discoursed with that minister on this subject, nor would ever give his consent to have one farthing of the said coin current here. And although it be a long time since I have given myself the trouble of conversing with people of titles or stations, yet I have been told by those who can take up with such amusements, that there is not a considerable person of the kingdom scrupulous in any sort to declare his opinion. But all this is needless to allege, when we consider, that the ruinous consequences of Wood's patent have been so strongly represented by both Houses of Parliament, by the Privy-council, the Lord Mayor and Aldermen of Dublin; by so many corporations; and the concurrence of the principal gentlemen in most counties at their quarter-sessions, without any regard to party, religion, or nation.

I conclude from hence, that the currency of these halfpence would, in the universal opinion of our people, be utterly destructive to this kingdom ; and, consequently, that it is every man's duty, not only to refuse this coin himself, but, as far as in him lies, to persuade others to do the like ; and whether this be done in private or in print, is all a case ; as no layman is forbidden to write or to discourse upon religious or moral subjects, although he may not do it in a pulpit, at least in our Church. Neither is this an affair of State, until authority shall think fit to declare it so, or, if you should understand it in that sense, yet you will please to consider, that I am not now preaching.

Therefore, I do think it my duty, since the Drapier will probably be no more heard of, so far to supply his place, as not to incur his fortune ; for I have learned from old experience that there are times wherein a man ought to be cautious as well as innocent. I therefore hope that, preserving both those characters, I may be allowed, by offering new arguments or enforcing old ones, to refresh the memory of my fellow-subjects, and keep up that good spirit raised among them, to preserve themselves from utter ruin by lawful means, and such as are permitted by his Majesty.

I believe you will please to allow me two propositions :

First, that we are a most loyal people ; and, secondly, that we are a free people, in the common acceptation of that word, applied to a subject under a limited monarch. I know very well that you and I did, many years ago, in discourse differ much in the presence of Lord Wharton about the meaning of that word *liberty*, with relation to Ireland. But, if you will not allow us to be a free people, there is only another appellation left, which I doubt my Lord Chief Justice Whitshed would call me to account for, if I venture to bestow : for I observed (and I shall never forget upon what occasion) the device upon his coach to be, *Libertas et natale solum*, at the very point of time when he was sitting in his court, and perjuring himself to betray both. . . .

I am heartily sorry that any writer should, in a cause so generally approved, give occasion to the government and council to charge him with paragraphs " highly reflecting upon his Majesty and his ministers ; tending to alienate the affections of his good subjects in England and Ireland from each other, and to promote sedition among the people." I must confess that, with many others, I thought he meant well, although he might have the failing of better writers, not to be always fortunate in the manner of expressing himself.

However, since the Drapier is but one man, I shall

think I do a public service by asserting that the rest of
my countrymen are wholly free from learning, out of his
pamphlets to reflect on the King or his ministers, and to
breed sedition. I solemnly declare, that I never once
heard the least reflection cast upon the King on the subject of Mr. Wood's coin: for in many discourses on this
matter, I do not remember his Majesty's name to be so
much as mentioned. As to the ministry in England,
the only two persons hinted at were the Duke of Grafton
and Mr. Walpole; the former, as I have heard you and
a hundred others affirm, declared, "that he never saw
the patent in favour of Mr. Wood before it was passed,"
although he was then Lord-Lieutenant; and therefore,
I suppose, everybody believes that his Grace has been
wholly unconcerned in it ever since. Mr. Walpole was
indeed supposed to be understood by the letter W. in
several newspapers, where it is said that some expressions fell from him not very favourable to the people of
Ireland, for the truth of which the kingdom is not to
answer, any more than for the discretion of the pub-
lishers. You observe, the Drapier wholly clears Mr.
Walpole of this charge by very strong arguments, and
speaks of him with civility.

I cannot deny myself to have been often present
where the company gave their opinion that Mr.

Walpole favoured Mr. Wood's projects, which I always contradicted, and for my own part never once opened my lips against that minister, either in mixed or particular meetings; and my reason for this reservedness was, because it pleased him in the Queen's time (I mean Queen Anne, of ever-blessed memory) to make a speech directly against me by name in the House of Commons, as I was told a very few minutes after, in the Court of Requests, by more than fifty members. . . .

But whatever unpleasing opinion some people might conceive of Mr. Walpole, on account of those half-pence, I dare boldly affirm it was entirely owing to Mr. Wood. Many persons of credit come from England, have affirmed to me and others, that they have seen letters under his hand, full of arrogance and insolence towards Ireland, and boasting of his favour with Mr. Walpole; which is highly probable; because he reasonably thought it for his interest to spread such a report, and because it is the known talent of low and little spirits, to have a great man's name perpetually in their mouths. Thus I have sufficiently justified the people of Ireland from learning any bad lesson out of the Drapier's pamphlets, with regard to his Majesty and his ministers; and therefore, if those papers were intended to sow sedition among us, God be thanked the seeds have fallen upon a very improper soil.

As to alienating the affections of the people of England and Ireland from each other, I believe the Drapier, whatever his intentions were, has left that matter just as he found it. I have lived long in both kingdoms, as well in country as in town ; and therefore take myself to be as well informed as most men, in the dispositions of each people toward the other. By the people, I understand here only the bulk of the common people : and I desire no lawyer may distort or extend my meaning. There is a vein of industry and parsimony, that runs through the whole people of England, which, added to the easiness of their rents, makes them rich and sturdy.

As to Ireland, they know little more of it than they do of Mexico : farther than that it is a country subject to the King of England, full of bogs, inhabited by wild Irish Papists, who are kept in awe by mercenary troops sent from thence : and their general opinion is, that it were better for England if this whole island were sunk into the sea ; for they have a tradition, that every forty years there must be a rebellion in Ireland.

I have seen the grossest suppositions passed upon them : " That the wild Irish were taken in toils ; but that in some time they would grow so tame as to eat out of your hands." I have been asked by hundreds, and particularly by my neighbours, your tenants at Pepper-harrow, "whether I had come from Ireland by sea?" and, upon the arrival of an Irishman to a country town, I have known crowds coming about him, and wondering to see him look so much better than themselves.

A gentleman, now in Dublin, affirms, "that, passing some months ago through Northampton, and finding the whole town in a flurry, with bells, bonfires, and illuminations; upon asking the cause, he was told that it was for joy that the Irish had submitted to receive Wood's halfpence." This, I think, plainly shows what sentiments that large town has of us; and how little they made it their own case; although they lie directly in our way to London, and therefore cannot but be frequently convinced that we have human shapes.

As to the people of this kingdom, they consist either of Irish Papists, who are as inconsiderable in point of power as the women and children; or of English Protestants, who love their brethren of that kingdom, although they may possibly sometimes complain when they think they are hardly used. However, I confess I do not see that it is of any great consequence, how the personal affec-

tions stand to each other, while the sea divides them
and while they continue in their loyalty to the same
prince. And yet I will appeal to you, whether those
from England have reason to complain when they come
hither in pursuit of their fortunes ? or, whether the
people of Ireland have reason to boast, when they go to
England upon the same design ? My second proposi-
tion was, that we of Ireland are a free people ; this, I
suppose, you will allow, at least with certain limitations
remaining in your own breast. However, I am sure it is
not criminal to affirm it ; because the words liberty and
property, as applied to the subject, are often mentioned
in both Houses of Parliament, as well as in yours and
other courts below ; whence it must follow, that the
people of Ireland do or ought to enjoy all the benefits
of the common and statute law : such as to be tried by
juries, to pay no money without their own consent as represented in Parliament, and the like. If this be so, and
if it be universally agreed that a free people cannot by law
be compelled to take any money in payment except gold
and silver, I do not see why any man should be hindered
from cautioning his countrymen against this coin of
William Wood, who is endeavouring by fraud to rob us
of that property which the laws have secured. . . .

Before I conclude, I cannot but observe that for several

months past there have more papers been written in this
town, such as they are, all upon the best public principle,
the love of our country, than perhaps has been known in
any other nation in so short a time.   I speak in general,
from the Drapier down to the maker of ballads ; and all
without any regard to the common motives of writers,
which are profit, favour, and reputation.   As to profit,
I am assured by persons of credit, that the best ballad
upon Mr. Wood will not yield above a groat to the
author ; and the unfortunate adventurer Harding[1] declares he never made the Drapier any present, except
one pair of scissors.   As to favour, whoever thinks to
make his court by opposing Mr. Wood, is not very
deep in politics ; and as to reputation, certainly no man
of worth and learning would employ his pen upon so
transitory a subject, and in so obscure a corner of the
world, to distinguish himself as an author, so that I look
upon myself, the Drapier, and my numerous brethren, to
be all true patriots in our several degrees.

All that the public can expect for the future is, only
to be sometimes warned to beware of Mr. Wood's halfpence, and to be referred for conviction to the Drapier's
reasons.   For a man of the most superior understanding
will find it impossible to make the best use of it while he

[1] The printer of the Drapier's Letters.

writes in constraint, perpetually softening, correcting, or blotting out expressions for fear of bringing his printer, or himself, under a prosecution from my Lord Chief Justice Whitshed. It calls to my remembrance the madman in "Don Quixote," who being soundly beaten by a weaver for letting a stone (which he always carried on his shoulder), fall upon a spaniel, apprehended that every cur he met was of the same species.

For these reasons I am convinced, that what I have now written will appear low and insipid ; but if it con- tributes in the least to preserve that union among us for opposing this fatal project of Mr. Wood, my pains will not be altogether lost.

I sent these papers to an eminent lawyer (and yet a man of virtue and learning into the bargain), who, after many alterations, returned them back, with assuring me that they are perfectly innocent ; without the least mix- ture of treason, rebellion, sedition, malice, disaffection, reflection, or wicked insinuation whatsoever.

If the bellman of each parish, as he goes his circuit, would cry out every night " Past twelve o'clock ; Beware of Wood's halfpence," it would probably cut off the occasion for publishing any more pamphlets ; provided that in country towns it were done upon market-days. For my own part, as soon as it shall be determined that

I

it is not against law, I will begin the experiment in the liberty of St. Patrick's ; and hope my example may be followed in the whole city. But if authority shall think fit to forbid all writings or discourses upon this subject, except such as are in favour of Mr. Wood, I will obey, as it becomes me ; only, when I am in danger of bursting, I will go and whisper among the reeds, not any reflection upon the wisdom of my countrymen, but only these few words, BEWARE OF WOOD'S HALFPENCE.

I am, with due respect,

Your most obedient, humble servant,

J. S.

SEVENTH LETTER

DID not appear till 1735. It appears to have been written during the first session in Lord Carteret's government. It is much more a start on a new course, than a continuation of the past struggle.

LETTER VII.

An Humble Address to Both Houses of Parliament.

BY M. B., DRAPIER.

"Multa gement plagasque superbi
  Victoris—"

I HAVE been told, that petitions and addresses, to either King or Parliament, are the right of every subject, provided they consist with that respect which is due to princes and great assemblies. Neither do I remember, that the modest proposals or opinions of private men have been ill-received, when they have not been delivered in the style of advice ; which is a presumption far from my thoughts. However, if proposals should be looked upon as too assuming, yet I hope every man may be suffered to declare his own and the nation's wishes. For instance ; I may be allowed to wish, that some farther laws were enacted for the advancement of trade ; for the improvement of agriculture, now strangely neglected, against the maxims of all wise nations ; for supplying the manifest defects in the acts concerning the plantation of trees ; for setting the poor to work ; and many others.

Upon this principle I may venture to affirm, it is the hearty wish of the whole nation, very few excepted, that the Parliament, in this session, would begin by strictly examining into the detestable fraud of one William Wood, now or late of London, hardwareman ; who illegally and clandestinely, as appears by your own votes and addresses, procured a patent in England for coining halfpence in that kingdom to be current here. This, I say, is the wish of the whole nation, very few excepted ; and upon account of those few, is more strongly and justly the wish of the rest ; those few con-sisting either of Wood's confederates, some obscure tradesmen, or certain bold UNDERTAKERS,[5] of weak judgment and strong ambition, who think to find their accounts in the ruin of the nation, by securing or advancing themselves. And because such men proceed upon a system of politics, to which I would fain hope you will be always utter strangers, I shall humbly lay it before you.

Be pleased to suppose me in a station of fifteen hundred pounds a year, salary and perquisites : and likewise possessed of 800*l.* a-year, real estate. Then suppose a destructive project to be set on foot; such for instance, as this of Wood ; which, if it succeed in all the consequences naturally to be expected from it, must sink the rents and wealth of the kingdom one half, although I am confident it would have done so five-sixths ; suppose, I conceive that the countenancing, or privately supporting, this project, will please those by whom I expect to be preserved or higher exalted ; nothing then remains, but to compute and balance my gain and my loss, and sum up the whole. I suppose

---

[5] Undertakers :—a name which was, in Charles II.'s time applied to those ministers who gained power by undertaking to carry through pet measures of the Crown. Swift here uses it ambiguously.

that I shall keep my employment ten years, not to mention the fair chance of a better.

This, at 1500*l.* a year, amounts in ten years to 15,000*l.* My estate, by the success of the said project, sinks 400*l.* a-year ; which, at twenty years' purchase, is but 8000*l.* ; so that I am a clear gainer of 7000*l.* upon the balance And during all that period I am possessed of power and credit, can gratify my favourites, and take vengeance on mine enemies. And if the project miscarry, my private merit is still entire. This arithmetic, as horrible as it appears, I knowingly affirm to have been practised and applied, in conjunctures whereon depended the ruin or safety of a nation ; although probably the charity and virtue of a senate will hardly be induced to believe, that there can be such monsters among mankind. And yet the wise Lord Bacon mentions a sort of people (I doubt the race is not yet extinct) who would "set a house on fire for the convenience of roasting their own eggs at the flame."

But whoever is old enough to remember, and has turned his thoughts to observe, the course of public affairs in this kingdom from the time of the Revolution, must acknow-ledge, that the highest points of interest and liberty have often been sacrificed to the avarice and ambition of par-ticular persons, upon the very principles and arithmetic that I have supposed. The only wonder is, how these artists were able to prevail upon numbers, and influence even public assemblies, to become instruments for effecting their execrable designs.

It is, I think, in all conscience, latitude enough for vice, if a man in station be al'owed to act injustice upon the usual principles of getting a bribe, wreaking his malice, serving his party, or consulting his preferment, while his wickedness terminates in the ruin only of particular persons; but to deliver up our whole country and every living soul who inhabits it, to certain destruction, has not, as I remember, been permitted by the most favourable casuists on the side of corruption.

It were far better, that all who have had the misfortune to be born in this kingdom, should be rendered incapable of holding any employment whatsoever above the degree of a constable (according to the scheme and intention of a great minister,[6] *gone to his own place*), than to live under the daily apprehension of a few false brethren among ourselves; because, in the former case, we should be wholly free from the danger of being betrayed, since none could then have impudence enough to pretend any public good. It is true, that in this desperate affair of the new halfpence, I have not heard of

_____

[6] The Earl of Sunderland.

any man above my own degree of a shopkeeper, to have
been hitherto so bold, as, in direct terms, to vindicate
the fatal project; although I have been told of some
very mollifying expressions which were used, and very
gentle expedients proposed and handed about, when it
first came under debate ; but since the eyes of the people
have been so far opened, that the most ignorant can
plainly see their own ruin in the success of Wood's
attempt, these grand compounders have been more
cautious. . . . In the small compass of my reading
(which, however, has been more extensive than is usual
to men of my inferior calling,) I have observed, that
grievances have always preceded supplies. And if ever
grievances had a title to such pre-eminence, it must be
this of Wood ; because it is not only the greatest grievance that any country could suffer, but a grievance of
such a kind, that, if it should take effect, would make it
impossible for us to give any supplies at all, except in
adulterate copper ; unless a tax were laid, for paying
the civil and military lists and the large pensions, with
real commodities instead of money. Which, however,
might be liable to some few objections, as well as difficulties ; for, although the common soldiers might be
content with beef, and mutton, and wool, and malt, and
leather, yet I am in some doubt as to the generals, the

colonels, the numerous pensioners, the civil officers and others, who all live in England upon Irish pay, as well as those few who reside among us only because they cannot help it.   There is one particular, which, although I have mentioned more than once in some of my former papers, yet I cannot forbear to repeat, and a little enlarge upon it ; because I do not remember to have read or heard of the like in.the history of any age or country, neither do I ever reflect upon it without the utmost astonishment.

After the unanimous addresses to his sacred Majesty, against the patent of Wood, from both Houses of Parliament, which are the three estates of the kingdom, and likewise an address from the Privy-council, to whom, under the chief governors, the whole administration is entrusted, the matter is referred to a committee of council in London.   Wood and his adherents are heard on one side ; and a few volunteers, without any trust or direction from hence, on the other.   The question, as I remember, chiefly turned upon the want of halfpence in Ireland.   Witnesses are called on the behalf of Wood, of what credit I have formerly shown.   Upon the issue, the patent is found good and legal ; all his Majesty's officers here, not excepting the military, commanded to be aiding and assisting to make it effectual ; the addresses of both Houses of Parliament, of the

Privy-council, and of the city of Dublin, the declarations of most counties and corporations throughout the kingdom, are altogether laid aside, as of no weight, consequence, or consideration whatsoever; and the whole kingdom of Ireland non-suited in default of appearance, as if it were a private case between John Doe, plaintiff, and William Roe, defendant.

With great respect to those honourable persons, the committee of council in London, I have not understood them to be our governors, councillors, or judges. Neither did our case turn at all upon the questions whether Ireland wanted halfpence or no. For there is no doubt, but we do want both halfpence, gold, and silver; and we have numberless other wants, and some that we are not so much as allowed to name, although they are peculiar to this nation; to which no other is subject, whom God has blessed with religion and laws, or any degree of soil and sunshine; but for what demerits on our side, I am altogether in the dark. But I do not remember that our want of halfpence was either affirmed or denied in any of our addresses or declarations against those of Wood. We alleged the fraudulent obtaining and executing of his patent; the baseness of his metal; and the prodigious sum to be coined, which might be increased by stealth, from foreign importation and his own counterfeits, as well as those at home ; whereby we must infallibly lose all our little gold and silver, and all our poor remainder of a very limited and discouraged trade. We urged, that the patent was passed without the least reference hither ; and without mention of any security given by Wood, to receive his own halfpence upon demand ; both which are contrary to all contrary proceedings in the like cases.

These, and many other arguments, we offered, but still the patent went on ; and at this day our ruin would have been half completed, if God in His mercy had not raised a universal detestation of these halfpence in the whole kingdom, with a firm resolution never to receive them ; since we are not under obligations to do so by any law, either human or divine.

But, in the name of God, and of all justice and pity, when the King's Majesty was pleased that this patent should pass, is it not to be understood that he conceived, believed, and intended it, as a gracious act for the good and benefit of his subjects, for the advantage of a great and fruitful kingdom ; of the most loyal kingdom upon earth, where no hand or voice was ever lifted up against him ; a kingdom, where the passage is not three hours from Britain ; and a kingdom where Papists have less

power and less land than in England? Can it be
denied or doubted that his Majesty's ministers understood and proposed the same end, the good of this
nation, when they advised the passing of this patent?
Can the person of Wood be otherwise regarded than as the
instrument, the mechanic, the head-workman, to prepare
his furnace, his fuel, his metal, and his stamps? If I
employ a shoe-boy, is it in view to his advantage, or
to my own convenience? I mention the person of
William Wood alone, because no other appears; and
we are not to reason upon surmises; neither would it
avail, if they had a real foundation. Allowing therefore
(for we cannot do less) that this patent for the coining
of halfpence was wholly intended by a gracious King,
and a wise public-spirited ministry, for the advantage of Ireland; yet when the whole kingdom to a
man, for whose good the patent was designed, do, upon
maturest consideration, universally join in openly
declaring, protesting, addressing, petitioning, against
these halfpence, as the most ruinous project that ever
was set on foot to complete the slavery and destruction
of a poor innocent country; is it, was it, can it, or will
it, ever be a question, not, whether such a kingdom, or
William Wood, should be a gainer; but whether such
a kingdom should be wholly undone, destroyed, sunk,

depopulated, made a scene of misery and desolation, for the sake of William Wood? God of His infinite mercy avert this dreadful judgment! And it is our universal wish, that God would put it into your hearts to be His instruments for so good a work.

For my own part, who am but one man, of obscure condition, I do solemnly declare, in the presence of Almighty God, that I will suffer the most ignominious and torturing death, rather than submit to receive this accursed coin, or any other that shall be liable to these objections, until they shall be forced upon me by a law of my own country ; and, if that shall ever happen, I will transport myself into some foreign land, and eat the bread of poverty among a free people.

Am I legally punishable for these expressions? shall another proclamation issue against me, because I presume to take my country's part against William Wood, where her final destruction is intended ? But, whenever you shall please to impose silence upon me, I will submit ; because I look upon your unanimous voice to be the voice of the nation ; and this I have been taught, and do believe, to be in some manner the voice of God. . . .

I have sometimes wondered upon what motives the peerage of England were so desirous to determine our controversies ; because I have been assured, and partly

know, that the frequent appeals from hence have been
very irksome to that illustrious body : and whoever has
frequented the Painted Chamber and Courts of Requests,
must have observed, that they are never so nobly filled
as when an Irish appeal is under debate.

The peers of Scotland, who are very numerous, were
content to reside in their castles and houses in that
bleak and barren climate ; and although some of them
made frequent journeys to London, yet I do not remember any of their greatest families, till very lately,
to have made England their constant habitation before
the Union ; or, if they did, I am sure it was generally to
their own advantage, and whatever they got was employed to cultivate and increase their own estates,
and by that means enrich themselves and their
country.

As to the great number of rich absentees under the
degree of peers, what particular ill-effects their absence
may have upon this kingdom, besides those already
mentioned, may perhaps be too tender a point to touch.
But whether those who live in another kingdom upon
great estates here, and have lost all regard to their own
country, farther than upon account of the revenues they
receive from it ; I say, whether such persons may not
be prevailed upon to recommend others to vacant seats,

who have no interest here except a precarious employment, and consequently can have no views but to preserve what they have got, or to be higher advanced ; this, I am sure, is a very melancholy question, if it be a question at all.

But, besides the prodigious profit which England receives by the transmittal thither of two-thirds of the revenues of this old kingdom, it has another mighty advantage, by making our country a receptacle, wherein to disburden themselves of their supernumerary pretenders to offices ; persons of second-rate merit in their own country, who, like birds of passage, most of them thrive and fatten here, and fly off when their credit and employments are at an end. So that Ireland may justly say, what Luther said of himself, POOR Ireland makes many rich !

If, amid all our difficulties, I should venture to assert that we have one great advantage, provided we could improve it as we ought, I believe most of my readers would be long in conjecturing what possible advantage could ever fall to our share. However, it is certain that all the regular seeds of party and faction among us are entirely rooted out, and if any new ones shall spring up, they must be of equivocal generation, without any seed at all, and will be justly imputed to a degree of stupidity beyond even what we have been ever charged with upon the score of our birthplace and climate.

The parties in this kingdom (including those of modern date) are, first, of those who have been charged or suspected to favour the Pretender ; and those who were zealous opposers of him. Secondly, of those who were for and against a toleration of Dissenters by law. Thirdly, of High and Low Church, or (to speak in the cant of the times) of Whig and Tory. And, fourthly, of court and country. If there be any more, they are beyond my observation or politics ; for, as to subaltern or occasional parties, they have been all derivations from the same originals.

Now it is manifest, that all these incitements to faction, party, and division, are wholly removed from among us. For, as to the Pretender, his cause is both desperate and obsolete. There are very few now alive who were men in his father's time, and in that prince's interest ; and in all others, the obligation of conscience has no place.[7] Even the Papists in general, of any substance or estates, and their priests almost universally, are what we call Whigs, in the sense which by that word

[7] The obligation arising from their having sworn allegiance to him.

is generally understood. They feel the smart, and see
the scars of their former wounds, and very well know,
that they must be made a sacrifice to the least attempts
toward a change ; although it cannot be doubted that
they would be glad to have their superstition restored,
under any prince whatsoever.

Secondly, the Dissenters are now tolerated by law;
neither do we observe any murmurs at present from that
quarter, except those reasonable complaints they make
of persecution, because they are excluded from civil
employments ; but their number being very small in
either House of Parliament, they are not yet in a situation to erect a party : because, however indifferent men
may be with regard to religion, they are now grown wise
enough to know that if such a latitude were allowed to
Dissenters, the few small employments left us in cities
and corporations would find other hands to lay hold on
them.

Thirdly, the dispute between High and Low Church
is now at an end; two-thirds of the bishops having been
promoted in this reign, and most of them from England,
who have bestowed all preferments in their gift to those
they could well confide in : the deaneries, all except
three, and many principal church-livings are in the
donation of the Crown, so that we already possess such

a body of clergy as will never engage in controversy upon that antiquated and exploded subject.

Lastly, as to court and country parties, so famous and avowed under most reigns in English Parliaments; this kingdom has not, for several years past, been a proper scene whereon to exercise such contentions, and is now less proper than ever; many great employments for life being in distant hands, and the reversions diligently watched and secured; the temporary ones of any inviting value are all bestowed elsewhere as fast as they drop, and the few remaining are of too low consideration to create contests about them, except among younger brothers, or tradesmen like myself. And therefore, to institute a court and country party, without materials would be a very new system in politics, and what I believe was never thought on before : nor, unless in a nation of idiots, can ever succeed ; for the most ignorant Irish cottager will not sell his cow for a groat.

Therefore I conclude, that all party and faction, with regard to public proceedings, are now extinguished in this kingdom ; neither does it appear in view how they can possibly revive, unless some new causes be administered ; which cannot be done without crossing the interests of those who are the greatest gainers by continuing the same measures. And general calamities,

K

without hope of redress, are allowed to be the great uniters of mankind.

However we may dislike the causes, yet this effect of begetting a universal discord among us, in all national debates, as well as in cities, corporations, and country neighbourhoods, may keep us at least alive, and in a condition to eat the little bread allowed us in peace and amity.

I have heard of a quarrel in a tavern, where all were at daggers drawing, till one of the company cried out, desiring to know the subject of the quarrel ; which, when none of them could tell, they put up their swords, sat down, and passed the rest of the evening in quiet. The former has been our case, I hope the latter will be so too ; that we shall sit down amicably together, at least until we have something that may give us a title to fall out, since nature has instructed even a brood of goslings to stick together, while the kite is hovering over their heads. . . .

THE ADDRESS TO THE JURY.

THIS piece, as its title expresses, was published when the bill against the printer was to be brought before the grand jury: it warned them of what was expected from them. Whiteshed, the Chief Justice, again attempted to browbeat the jury, but in vain. The bill was thrown out: and the Chief Justice could only show his resentment by dissolving the Grand Jury. Whiteshed was so ridiculed that the vexation he suffered was thought to have shortened his life.

Seasonable Advice to the Grand Jury.

Concerning the bill preparing against the printer of the Drapier's fourth letter.

November 11th, 1724.

SINCE a bill is preparing for the grand jury to find against the printer of the Drapier's last letter, there are several things maturely to be considered by those gentlemen before they determine upon it.

First, they are to consider, that the author of the said

pamphlet did write three other discourses on the same subject, which, instead of being censured, were universally approved by the whole nation, and were allowed to have raised and continued that spirit among us, which has hitherto kept out Wood's coin ; for all men will grant, that if those pamphlets had not been written, his coin must have overrun the nation some months ago.

Secondly, it is to be considered, that this pamphlet, against which a proclamation has been issued, is written by the same author : that nobody ever doubted the innocence and goodness of his design ; that he appears, through the whole tenour of it, to be a loyal subject to his Majesty, and devoted to the House of Hanover, and declares himself in a manner peculiarly zealous against the Pretender. And if such a writer, in four several treatises on so nice a subject, where a royal patent is concerned, and where it was necessary to speak of England and of liberty, should in one or two places happen to let fall an inadvertent expression, it would be hard to condemn him, after all the good he has done, especially when we consider that he could have no possible design in view, either of honour or profit, but purely the GOOD of his country.

Thirdly, it ought to be well considered, whether any one expression in the said pamphlet be really liable to a just exception, much less to be found "wicked, malicious, seditious, reflecting upon his Majesty and his ministry," &c.

The two points in that pamphlet, which it is said the prosecutors intend chiefly to fix on, are, first, where the author mentions the penner of the King's answer. First, it is well known his Majesty is not master of the English tongue ; and therefore it is necessary that some other person should be employed to pen what he has to say or write in that language. Secondly, his Majesty's answer is not in the first person, but in the third. It is not said, WE are concerned, or OUR royal predecessors ; but HIS MAJESTY is concerned, and HIS royal pre- decessors. By which it is plain, these are properly not the words of his Majesty, but supposed to be taken from him, and transmitted hither by one of his ministers. Thirdly, it will be easily seen, that the author of the pamphlet delivers his sentiments upon this particular with the utmost caution and respect, as any impartial reader will observe.

The second paragraph, which it is said will be taken notice of as a motive to find the bill, is what the author says of Ireland's being a dependent kingdom ; he explains all the dependence he knows of, which is a law made in Ireland, whereby it is enacted, "that whoever

is King of England shall be King of Ireland." Before
this explanation be condemned, and the bill found upon
it, it would be proper that some lawyers should fully
inform the jury what other law there is, either statute or
common, for this dependency; and if there be no law,
there is no transgression.

The fourth thing very maturely to be considered by
the jury, is, what influence their finding the bill may
have upon the kingdom; the people in general find no
fault in the Drapier's last book, any more than in the
three former; and therefore, when they hear it is condemned by a grand jury of Dublin, they will conclude it
is done in favour of Wood's coin; they will think we of
this town have changed our minds, and intend to take
those halfpence, and therefore it will be in vain for them
to stand out: so that the question comes to this, which
will be of the worst consequence?—to let pass one or
two expressions, at the worst only unwary, in a book
written for the public service; or to leave a free, open
passage for Wood's brass to overrun us, by which we
shall be undone for ever. The fifth thing to be considered is, that the members of the grand jury, being
merchants and principal shopkeepers, can have no suitable temptation offered them as a recompense for the
mischief they will do and suffer by letting-in this coin;

nor can be at any loss or danger by rejecting the bill.
They do not expect any employments in the State, to
make up in their own private advantages the destruction
of their country ; whereas those who go about to advise,
entice, or threaten them to find that bill, have great
employments, which they have a mind to keep, or to
get a greater; as it was likewise the case of all those
who signed the proclamation to have the author prosecuted.   And therefore it is known, that his grace the
Lord Archbishop of Dublin, so renowned for his piety
and wisdom, and love of his country, absolutely refused
to condemn the book or the author.

Lastly, it ought to be considered what consequence
the finding of the bill may have upon a poor man
perfectly innocent.   I mean the printer.   A lawyer
may pick out expressions, and make them liable to exception, where no other man is able to find any.   But
how can it be supposed that an ignorant printer can be
such a critic ?   He knew the author's design was honest
and approved by the whole kingdom : he advised with
friends, who told him there was no harm in the book,
and he could see none himself : it was sent him in an
unknown hand ; but the same in which he received the
three former.   He and his wife have offered to take
their oaths that they knew not the author, and therefore,

to find a bill that may bring punishment upon the innocent, will appear very hard, to say no worse. For it
will be impossible to find the author, unless he will
please to discover himself; although I wonder he ever
concealed his name; but I suppose what he did at first
out of modesty, he continues to do out of prudence.
God protect us and him!

I will conclude all with a fable ascribed to Demos-
thenes. He had served the people of Athens with
great fidelity in the station of an orator, when, upon a
certain occasion, apprehending to be delivered over to his
enemies, he told the Athenians, his countrymen, the
following story: Once upon a time the wolves desired
a league with the sheep, upon this condition, that the
cause of the strife might be taken away, which was the
shepherds and mastiffs : this being granted, the wolves,
without all fear, made havoc of the sheep.

SWIFT'S DESCRIPTION OF QUILCA.

THE summers of 1724 and 1725 were spent in this country-seat, which his friend Sheridan built for himself amongst the wildest of the Cavan heaths. Quilca stood near a little lake surrounded by trees. Here Sheridan tried a revival of the Roman chariot-races; the slope close by the lake was used for a theatre; the place is redolent with memories of Swift, who loved the place, though he perpetuated in verse the memory of its disorders, its dilapidations, and the general shortcomings, in which it reflected its owner's character and that of his scolding wife.

_____

THE BLUNDERS, DEFICIENCIES, DISTRESSES, AND MISFORTUNES OF QUILCA.

Proposed to contain one-and-twenty volumes in quarto.

Begun April 20, 1724. To be continued weekly, if due encouragement be given.

_____

BUT one lock and a half in the whole house.

The key of the garden-door lost.

The empty bottles all uncleanable.

The vessels for drink very few and leaky.

The new house going to ruin before it is finished.

One hinge of the street-door broke off, and the people forced to go out and come in at the back-door.

The door of the Dean's bed-chamber full of large chinks.

The beaufet letting in so much wind that it almost blows out the candles.

The Dean's bed threatening every night to fall under him.

The little table loose and broken in the joints.

The passages open overhead, by which the cats pass continually into the cellar, and eat the victuals, for which one was tried, condemned, and executed by the sword.

The large table in a very tottering condition.

But one chair in the house fit for sitting on, and that in a very ill state of health.

The kitchen perpetually crowded with savages.

Not a bit of mutton to be had in the country.

Want of beds, and a mutiny thereupon among the servants, until supplied from Kells.

An egregious want of all the most common necessary utensils.

Not a bit of turf in this cold weather; and Mrs. Johnson and the Dean in person, with all their servants, forced to assist at the bog, in gathering up the wet bottoms of old clumps.

The grate in the ladies' bedchamber broke, and forced to be removed, by which they were compelled to be without fire, the chimney smoking intolerably; and the Dean's great-coat was employed to stop the wind from coming down the chimney, without which expedient they must have been starved to death.

A messenger sent a mile to borrow an old broken tun-dish.

Bottles stopped with bits of wood and tow, instead of corks.

Not one utensil for a fire, except an old pair of tongs, which travels through the house, and is likewise employed to take the meat out of the pot, for want of a flesh-fork.

Every servant an arrant thief as to victuals and drink, and every comer and goer as arrant a thief of everything he or she can lay their hands on.

The spit blunted with poking into bogs for timber, and tears the meat to pieces.

Bellum atque fœminam; or a kitchen war between nurse and a nasty crew of both sexes; she to preserve order and cleanliness, they to destroy both ; and they generally are conquerors.

April 28.   This morning the great fore-door quite open, dancing backward and forward with all its weight upon the lower hinge, which must have been broken if the Dean had not accidentally come and relieved it.

A great hole in the floor of the ladies' chamber, every hour hazarding a broken leg.

Two iron spikes erect on the Dean's bedstead, by which he is in danger of a broken shin at rising and going to bed.

The ladies' and Dean's servants growing fast into the manners and thieveries of the natives ; the ladies them- selves very much corrupted; the Dean perpetually storm- ing, and in danger of either losing all his flesh, or sinking into barbarity for the sake of peace.

Mrs. Dingley full of cares for herself, and blunders and negligence for her friends.   Mrs. Johnson sick and helpless.   The Dean deaf and fretting ; the lady's maid awkward and clumsy; Robert lazy and forgetful ; William a pragmatical, ignorant, and conceited puppy ; Robin and nurse the two great and only supports of the family.

Bellum lactæum ; or the milky battle, fought between the Dean and the crew of Quilca ; the latter insisting on

their privilege of not milking till eleven in the forenoon :
whereas Mrs. Johnson wanted milk at eight for her
health. In this battle the Dean got the victory ; but the
crew of Quilca begin to rebel again ; for it is this day
almost ten o'clock, and Mrs. Johnson has not got her
milk.

A proverb on the laziness and lodgings of the servants :
" The worse their sty—the longer they lie."

Two great holes in the wall of the ladies' bedchamber,
just at the back of the bed, and one of them directly
behind Mrs. Johnson's pillow, either of which would
blow out a candle in the calmest day.

ANSWER TO A PAPER,

CALLED

A Memorial of the poor Inhabitants, Tradesmen, and Labourers of the Kingdom of Ireland.[1]

Dublin, *March 25th*, 1738.

SIR,

I received a paper from you, whoever you are, printed without any name of author or printer, and sent, I suppose, to me among others, without any particular distinction. It contains a complaint of the dearness of corn, and some schemes for making it cheaper which I cannot approve of.

But pray permit me, before I go farther, to give you a short history of the steps by which we arrived at this hopeful situation.

It was, indeed, the shameful practice of too many Irish farmers, to wear out their ground with ploughing; while, either through poverty, laziness, or ignorance, they neither took care to measure it as they ought, nor

---

[1] The memorial was written by Sir John Browne.

gave time to any part of the land to recover itself; and when their leases were near expiring, being assured that their landlords would not renew, they ploughed even the meadows, and made such havoc, that their landlords were considerable sufferers by it.

This gave birth to that abominable race of graziers, who, upon expiration of the farmers' leases, were ready to engross great quantities of land; and the gentlemen having been often before ill paid, and their land worn out of heart, were too easily tempted, when a rich grazier made an offer to take all their land, and give them security for payment. Thus a vast tract of land, where twenty or thirty farmers lived, together with their cottagers and labourers in their several cabins, became all desolate, and easily managed by one or two herds-men and their boys; whereby the master grazier, with little trouble, seized to himself the livelihood of a hundred people.

It must be confessed, that the farmers were justly punished for their knavery, brutality, and folly. But neither are the squires and landlords to be excused; for to them is owing the depopulating of the country, the vast number of beggars, and the ruin of those few sorry improvements we had. That farmers should be limited in ploughing is very reasonable, and practised in England, and might have easily been done here by penal clauses in their leases ; but to deprive them, in a manner, altogether from tilling their lands, was a most stupid want of thinking.

Had the farmers been confined to plough a certain quantity of land, with a penalty of ten pounds an acre for whatever they exceeded, and farther limited for the three or four last years of their leases, all this evil· had been prevented ; the nation would have saved a million of money, and been more populous by above two hundred thousand souls.

For a people, denied the benefit of trade, to manage their lands in such a manner as to produce nothing but what they are forbidden to trade with, or only such things as they can neither export nor manufacture to advantage, is an absurdity that a wild Indian would be ashamed of; especially when we add, that we are content to purchase this hopeful commerce, by sending to foreign markets for our daily bread.

The grazier's employment is to feed great flocks of sheep, or black-cattle, or both. With regard to sheep, as folly is usually accompanied with perverseness, so it is here. There is something so monstrous to deal in a commodity (farther than for our own use), which we are not allowed to export manufactured, nor even unmanufactured, but to one certain country, and only to some few ports in that country ; there is, I say, something so sottish, that it wants a name in our language to express it by, and the good of it is, that the more sheep we have, the fewer human creatures are left to wear the wool, or eat the flesh.

Ajax was mad when he mistook a flock of sheep for his enemies ; but we shall never be sober until we have the same way of thinking.

The other part of the grazier's business is, what we call black-cattle, producing hides, tallow, and beef for exportation : all which are good and useful commodities, if rightly managed. But it seems the greatest part of the hides are sent out raw, for want of bark to tan them ; and that want will daily grow stronger, for I doubt the new project of tanning without it is at an end.

Our beef, I am afraid, still continues scandalous in foreign markets, for the old reasons ; but our tallow, for anything I know, may be good. However, to bestow the whole kingdom on beef and mutton, and thereby drive out half the people who should eat their share, and force the rest to send sometimes as far as Egypt for bread to eat with it, is a most peculiar and distinguished piece of public economy, of which I have no comprehension.

L

I know very well that our ancestors the Scythians, and their posterity, our kinsmen the Tartars, lived upon the blood, and milk, and raw flesh of their cattle, without one grain of corn ; but I confess myself so degenerate, that I am not easy without bread to my victuals. . . .

Now, sir, to return more particularly to you and your memorial. A hundred thousand barrels of wheat, you say, should be imported hither : and ten thousand pounds, premium to the importers. Have you looked into the purse of the nation ?

I am no Commissioner of the Treasury ; but am well assured that the whole running cash would not supply you with a sum to purchase so much corn, which, only at twenty shillings a barrel, will be a hundred thousand pounds ; and ten thousand more for the premium. But you will traffic for your corn with other goods ; and where are those goods ? if you had them, they are all engaged to pay the rents of absentees, and other occasions in London, besides a huge balance of trade this year against us. Will foreigners take our bankers' paper ? I suppose they will value it at little more than so much a quire. Where are these rich farmers and engrossers of corn, in so bad a year, and so little sowing. You are in pain for two shillings premium, and forget the twenty shillings for the price ; find me out the latter, and I will engage for the former.

Your scheme for a tax for raising such a sum is all visionary, and owing to a great want of knowledge in the miserable state of this nation. Tea, coffee, sugar, spices, wine, and foreign clothes, are the particulars you mention upon which this tax should be raised. I will allow the two first; because they are unwholesome ; and the last, because I should be glad if they were all burned : but I beg you will leave us our wine to make us awhile forget our misery, or give your tenants leave to plough for barley. But I will tell you a secret, which I learned many years ago from the commissioners of the customs in London : they said, when any commodity appeared to be taxed above a moderate rate, the consequence was, to lessen that branch of the revenue by one half; and one of those gentlemen pleasantly told me, that the mistake of parliaments, on such occasions, was owing to an error of computing two and two to make four, whereas, in the business of laying impositions, two and two never made more than one ; which happens by lessening the import, and the strong temptation of running such goods as paid high duties at least in this kingdom. . . .

You are concerned how strange and surprising it

would be in foreign parts to hear that the poor were starving in a RICH country, &c. Are you in earnest ? Is Ireland the rich country you mean ? Or are you insulting our poverty ? Were you ever out of Ireland ? Or were you ever in it till of late ? You may probably have a good employment, and are saving all you can to purchase a good estate in England.

But by talking so familiarly of one hundred and ten thousand pounds, by a tax upon a few commodities, it is plain you are either naturally or affectedly ignorant of our present condition : or else you would know and allow, that such a sum is not to be raised here, without a general excise ; since, in proportion to our wealth, we pay already in taxes more than England ever did in the height of war. And when you have brought over your corn, who will be the buyers ?—most certainly not the poor, who will not be able to purchase the twentieth part of it.

Sir, upon the whole, your paper is a very crude piece, liable to more objections than there are lines ; but I think your meaning is good, and so far you are pardonable.

If you will propose a general contribution for sup- porting the poor in potatoes and butter-milk till the new corn comes in, perhaps you may succeed better, because the thing at least is possible ; and I think if our brethren

in England would contribute upon this emergency, out
of the million they gain from us every year, they would
do a piece of justice as well as charity. In the meantime, go and preach to your own tenants to fall to the
plough as fast as they can, and prevail with your neighbouring squires to do the same with theirs; or else die
with the guilt of having driven away half the inhabitants,
and starving the rest.

But why all this concern for the poor? We want
them not, as the country is now managed; they may
follow thousands of their leaders, and seek their bread
abroad. Where the plough has no work, one family
can do the business of fifty, and you may send away
the other forty-nine. An admirable piece of husbandry,
never known or practised by the wisest nations, who
erroneously thought people to be the riches of a country!

If so wretched a state of things would allow it, me-
thinks I could have a malicious pleasure, after all the
warning I have in vain given the public, at my own
peril, for several years past, to see the consequences and
events answering in every particular. I pretend to no
sagacity; what I writ was little more than what I had
discoursed to several persons, who were generally of my
opinion, and it was obvious to every common understanding that such effects must needs follow from such

causes—a fair issue of things begun upon party rage, while some sacrificed the public to fury, and others to ambition; while a spirit of faction and oppression reigned in every part of the country, where gentlemen, instead of consulting the ease of their tenants, or cultivating their lands, were worrying one another upon points of Whig and Tory, of High Church and Low Church, which no more concerned them than the long and famous controversy of strops for razors : while agriculture was wholly discouraged, and consequently half the farmers and labourers, and poorer tradesmen forced to beggary or banishment. "Wisdom crieth in the streets : Because I have called on you ; I have stretched out my hand, and no man regarded ; but ye have set at nought all my counsels, and would none of my reproof; I also will laugh at your calamity, and mock when your fear cometh."

I have now done with your Memorial, and freely excuse your mistakes, since you appear to write as a stranger, and as of a country which is left at liberty to enjoy the benefits of nature, and to make the best of those advantages which God has given it, in soil, climate, and situation.

MAXIMS CONTROLLED.

THE heading of this tract would imply that the theories of political economy have no application to Ireland. Here he shows, one by one, how the ordinary rules that guide us in regard to other nations are utterly fallacious when applied to Ireland. What strikes us most in all these tracts is the deliberate incisiveness of their irony, the despairing bitterness that gives them finish and completeness.

MAXIMS CONTROULED IN IRELAND.

The Truth of Maxims in State and Government examined with reference to Ireland.

Written in 1724.

THERE are certain maxims of State, founded upon long observation and experience, drawn from the constant practice of the wisest nations, and from the very principles of government, nor even controuled by any writer on politics. Yet all these maxims do necessarily presuppose a kingdom, or commonwealth, to have the same natural rights common to the rest of mankind, who have entered into civil society; for if we could conceive a nation where each of the inhabitants had but one eye, one leg, and one hand, it is plain, before you could institute them into a republic, that an allowance must be made for those material defects wherein they differed from other mortals. Or, imagine a legislature forming a system for the government of bedlam, and, proceeding upon the maxim that man is a sociable animal, should draw them out of their cells, and form them into corporations or general assemblies; the consequence might probably be that they would fall foul on each other, or burn the house over their own heads.

Of the like nature are innumerable errors committed by crude and short thinkers, who reason upon general topics, without the least allowance for the most important circumstances, which quite alter the nature of the case.

This has been the fate of those small dealers who are every day publishing their thoughts, either on paper or in their assemblies, for improving the trade of Ireland, and referring us to the practice and example of England, Holland, France, or other nations.

I shall, therefore, examine certain maxims of government, which generally pass for uncontrouled in the world, and consider how far they will suit with the present condition of this kingdom. First, It is affirmed by wise men that the dearness of things necessary for life, in a fruitful country, is a certain sign of wealth and great commerce ; for when such necessaries are dear, it must absolutely follow that money is cheap and plentiful.

But this is manifestly false in Ireland, for the following reason. Some years ago, the species of money here did probably amount to six or seven hundred thousand pounds ; and I have good cause to believe that our remittances then did not much exceed the cash brought in to us. But, by the prodigious discouragements we have since received in every branch of our trade, by the frequent enforcement and rigorous execution of the Navigation-act—the tyranny of under custom-house officers—the yearly addition of absentees—the payments to regiments abroad, to civil and military officers residing in England—the unexpected sudden demands of great sums from the treasury—and some other drains of perhaps as great consequence—we now see ourselves reduced to a state (since we have no friends) of being pitied by our enemies ; at least, if our enemies were of such a kind as to be capable of any regard towards us except of hatred and contempt.

Forty years are now passed since the Revolution, when the contention of the British Empire was, most unfortunately for us, and altogether against the usual course of such mighty changes in government, decided in the least important nation ; but with such ravages and ruin executed on both sides, as to leave the kingdom a desert, which in some sort it still con‐ tinues.

Neither did the long rebellions in 1641, make half such a destruction of houses, plantations, and personal wealth, in both kingdoms, as two years' campaigns did in ours, by fighting England's battles.

By slow degrees, as by the gentle treatment we received under two auspicious reigns,[1] we grew able to live without running in debt.

Our absentees were but few ; we had great indulgence in trade, and a considerable share in employments of Church and State ; and while the short leases continued, which were let some years after the war ended, tenants paid their rents with ease and cheerfulness, to the great regret of their landlords, who had taken up a spirit of opposition that is not easily removed. And although in these short leases, the rent was gradually to increase

[1] Ireland was, for political reasons, much favoured by the Crown, during the reigns of Charles II. and James II.

after short periods, yet, as soon as the terms elapsed, the land was let to the highest bidder, most commonly without the least effectual clause for building or planting. Yet, by many advantages, which this island then possessed, and has since utterly lost, the rents of land still grew higher upon every lease that expired, till they have arrived at the present exorbitance; when the frog, over-swelling himself, burst at last.

With the price of land, of necessity rose that of corn and cattle, and all other commodities that farmers deal in; hence likewise, obviously, the rates of all goods and manufactures among shopkeepers, the wages of servants, and hire of labourers. But although our miseries came on fast, with neither trade nor money left; yet neither will the landlord abate in his rent, nor can the tenant abate in the price of what the rest must be paid with, nor any shopkeeper, tradesman, or labourer live, at lower expense for food and clothing, than he did before.

I have been the larger upon this first head, because the same observations will clear up and strengthen a good deal of what I shall affirm upon the rest.

The second maxim of those who reason upon trade and government, is, to assert that low interest is a certain sign of great plenty of money in a nation, for which, as in many other articles, they produce the examples of Holland and England. But, with relation to Ireland, this maxim is likewise entirely false.

There are two reasons for the lowness of interest in any country. First, that which is usually alleged, the great plenty of species ; and this is obvious. The second is, want of trade, which seldom falls under common observation, although it be equally true, for, where trade is altogether discouraged, there are few borrowers. In those countries where men can employ a large stock, the young merchant, whose fortune may be four or five hundred pounds, will venture to borrow as much more, and can afford a reasonable interest. Neither is it easy, at this day, to find many of those, whose business reaches to employ even so inconsiderable a sum, except among the importers of wine, who, as they have most part of the present trade in these parts of Ireland in their hands, so they are the most exorbitant, exacting fraudulent dealers, that ever trafficked in any nation, and are making all possible speed to ruin both them-selves and the nation.

From this defect of gentlemen's not knowing how to dispose of their ready money, arises the high purchase of land, which in all other countries is reckoned a sign of wealth. For, the frugal squires, who live below their incomes, have no other way to dispose of their savings but by mortgage or purchase, by which the rates of land must naturally increase ; and if this trade continues long, under the uncertainty of rents, the landed men of ready money will find it more for their advantage to send their cash to England, and place it in the funds ; which I myself am determined to do, the first considerable sum I shall be master of.

It has likewise been a maxim among politicians, "That the great increase of buildings in the metropolis, argues a flourishing state." But this, I confess, has been controuled from the example of London ; when, by the long and annual parliamentary session, such a number of senators with their families, friends, adherents, and expectants, draw such prodigious numbers to that city, that the old hospitable custom of lords and gentlemen living in their ancient seats among their tenants, is almost lost in England ; is laughed out of doors ; insomuch that, in the middle of summer, a legal House of Lords and Commons might be brought in a few hours to London, from their country villas within twelve miles round.

The case in Ireland is yet somewhat worse : for the absentees of great estates, who, if they lived at home, would have many rich retainers in their neighbourhoods, have learned to rack their lands, and shorten their leases,

as much as any residing squire ; and the few remaining
of those latter, having some vain hope of employments
for themselves, or their children, and discouraged by the
beggarliness and thievery of their own miserable farmers
and cottagers, or seduced by the vanity of their wives,
on pretence of their children's education (whereof the
fruits are so apparent), together with that most wonderful, and yet more unaccountable zeal, for a seat in their
assembly, though at some years' purchase of their whole,
estates : these, and some other motives, have drawn
such concourse to this beggarly city, that the dealers of
the several branches of building have found out all the
commodious and inviting places for erecting new houses ;
while fifteen hundred of the old ones, which is a seventh
part of the whole city, are said to be left uninhabited,
and falling to ruin.   Their method is the same with that
which was first introduced by Dr. Barebone at London,
who died a bankrupt.   The mason, the bricklayer, the
carpenter, the slater, and the glazier, take a lot of ground,
club to build one or more houses, unite their credit, their
stock, and their money ; and when their work is finished
sell it to the best advantage they can.   But, as it often
happens, and more every day, that their fund will not
answer half their design, they are forced to undersell it
at the first story, and are all reduced to beggary.   Inso-

much, that I know a certain fanatic brewer, who is re-ported to have some hundreds of houses in this town, is said to have purchased the greatest part of them at half value from ruined undertakers ; has intelligence of all new houses where the finishing is at a stand, takes advantage of the builders' distress, and, by the advantage of ready money, gets fifty *per cent.* at least for his bargain.

It is another undisputed maxim in government, " That people are the riches of a nation ;" which is so uni-versally granted, that it will be hardly pardonable to bring it into doubt. And I will grant it to be so far true, even in this island, that if we had the African custom, or privilege, of selling our useless bodies for slaves to foreigners, it would be the most useful branch of our trade, by ridding us of a most unsupportable burden, and bringing us money in the stead. But, in our present situation, at least five children in six who are born, lie a dead weight upon us, for want of employ-ment. And a very skilful computer assured me, that above one half of the souls in this kingdom supported themselves by begging and thievery ; two-thirds whereof would be able to get their bread in any other country upon earth. Trade is the only incitement to labour ; where that fails, the poorer native must either beg, steal or starve, or be forced to quit his country. This has

made me often wish, for some years past, that instead of
discouraging our people from seeking foreign soil, the
public would rather pay for transporting all our unnecessary mortals, whether Papists or Protestants, to
America ; as drawbacks are sometimes allowed for exporting commodities, where a nation is overstocked.   I
confess myself to be touched with very sensible pleasure,
when I hear of a mortality in any country parish or
village, where the wretches are forced to pay for a filthy
cabin, and two ridges of potatoes, treble the worth ;
brought up to steal or beg, for want of work ; to whom
death would be the best thing to be wished for on
account both of themselves and the public.

Among all taxes imposed by the legislature, those
upon luxury are universally allowed to be the most
equitable, and beneficial to the subject ; and the com-
monest reasoner on government might fill a volume with
arguments on the subject.   Yet here again, by the
singular fate of Ireland, this maxim is utterly false ; and
the putting of it in practice may have such a pernicious
consequence, as, I certainly believe, the thoughts of pro-
posers were not able to reach.

The miseries we suffer by our absentees, are of a far
more extensive nature than seems to be commonly
understood.   I must vindicate myself to the reader so

far, as to declare solemnly, that what I shall say of those
lords and squires, does not arise from the least regard
I have for their understandings, their virtues, or their
persons: for, although I have not the honour of the
least acquaintance with any one among them (my
ambition not soaring so high), yet I am too good a witness of the situation they have been in for thirty years
past; the veneration paid them by the people, the high
esteem they are in among the prime nobility and gentry,
the particular marks of favour and distinction they receive from the Court; the weight and consequence of
their interest, added to their great zeal and application
for preventing any hardships their country might suffer
from England, wisely considering that their own fortunes
and honours were embarked in the same bottom.

M

A SHORT VIEW OF THE STATE OF
IRELAND, 1727.

HERE, Swift catalogues in regular order the possible
adjuncts and conditions of prosperity, and shows how
the very negative of each is present in Ireland. "If we
flourish, it is against every law of nature and reason :
like the thorn of Glastonbury, which blossoms in the
midst of winter." He draws a fanciful picture of what
Ireland might seem to a stranger, favoured as she is by
nature ; but breaks from it in despair. All his tracts
have one end and aim : "Be independent." Law
cannot help ; theory is futile ; English selfishness is
great. Whatever you get will be by self-assertion and
by that alone. Swift was acquainted with the current
nostrums, which he despised. He saw the evil lay
deeper, and that it could be cured only by giving to
Ireland the motive power of independence. He kindled
her energy by plain bald statements, withering sarcasm,
derisive scorn, and the fiercest indignation. The sarcasm
and indignation are for the English selfishness ; the
scorn for Irish imbecility and weakness.

A Short View of the State of Ireland, 1727.

I AM assured, that it has for some time been practised as a method of making men's court, when they are asked about the rate of lands, the abilities of the tenants, the state of trade and manufacture in this kingdom, and how their rents are paid ; to answer, that in their neighbourhood all things are in a flourishing condition, the rent and purchase of land every day increasing. And if a gentleman happen to be a little more sincere in his representation, besides being looked on as not well-affected, he is sure to have a dozen contradictors at his elbow. I think it is no manner of secret, why these questions are so cordially asked, or so obligingly answered.

But since, with regard to the affairs of this kingdom, I have been using all endeavours to subdue my indignation, to which indeed I am not provoked by any personal interest, not being the owner of one spot of ground in the whole island ; I shall only enumerate, by rules generally known, and never contradicted, what are the true causes of any country's flourishing and growing rich ; and then examine what effects arise from those causes in the kingdom of Ireland.

The first cause of a kingdom's thriving is, the fruit-

fulness of the soil to produce the necessaries and conveniences of life ; not only sufficient for the inhabitants,
but for exportation into other countries.

The second is, the industry of the people, in working
up all their native commodities to the last degree of
manufacture.

The third is, the conveniency of safe ports and
havens, to carry out their own goods as much manufactured, and bring in those of others as little manufactured
as the nature of mutual commerce will allow.

The fourth is, that the natives should, as much as
possible, export and import their goods in vessels of
their own timber, made in their own country.

The fifth is, the privilege of a free trade in all foreign
countries which will permit them, except those who are
in war with their own prince or State.

The sixth is, by being governed only by laws made
with their own consent ; for otherwise they are not a
free people.   And therefore all appeals for justice, or
applications for favour or preferment, to another country,
are so many grievous impoverishments.

The seventh is, by improvement of land, encouragement of agriculture, and thereby increasing the number
of their people ; without which any country, however
blessed by nature, must continue poor.

The eighth is, the residence of the prince, or chief administrator of the civil power.

The ninth is, the concourse of foreigners, for education, curiosity, or pleasure, or as to a general mart of trade.

The tenth is, by disposing all offices of honour, profit, or trust, only to the natives ; or at least with very few exceptions, where strangers have long inhabited the country, and are supposed to understand and regard the interests of it as their own.

The eleventh is, when the rents of land and profits of employment are spent in the country which produced them, and not in another; the former of which will certainly happen where the love of our native country prevails.

The twelfth is, by the public revenues being all spent and employed at home, except on the occasions of a foreign war.

The thirteenth is, where the people are not obliged unless they find it for their own interest or conveniency, to receive any moneys, except of their own coinage by a public mint, after the manner of all civilized nations.

The fourteenth is, a disposition of the people of a country to wear their own manufactures, and import as few incitements to luxury, either in clothes, furniture, food, or drink, as they can possibly live conveniently without.

There are many other causes of a nation's thriving, which I at present cannot recollect ; but without advantage from at least some of these, after turning my thoughts a long time, I am not able to discover whence our wealth proceeds, and therefore would gladly be better informed.   In the meantime, I will here examine what share falls to Ireland of these causes, or of the effects and consequences.

It is not my intention to complain, but barely to relate facts ; and the matter is not of small importance. For it is allowed, that a man who lives in a solitary house, far from help, is not wise in endeavouring to acquire in the neighbourhood the reputation of being rich ; because those who come for gold, will go off with pewter and brass, rather than return empty : and in the common practice of the world, those who possess most wealth, make the least parade ; which they leave to others, who have nothing else to bear them out in showing their faces on the Exchange.

As to the first cause of a nation's riches, being the fertility of the soil, as well as temperature of the climate, we have no reason to complain ; for, although the quantity of unprofitable land in this kingdom, reckoning

bog and rock and barren mountain, be double in proportion to what it is in England ; yet the native productions, which both kingdoms deal in, are very near
on an equality in point of goodness, and might, with
the same encouragement, be as well manufactured. I
except mines and minerals ; in some of which, however,
we are only defective in point of skill and industry. In
the second, which is the industry of the people, our
misfortune is not altogether owing to our own fault,
but to a million of discouragements.

The conveniency of ports and havens, which nature
has bestowed so liberally on this kingdom, is of no
more use to us than a beautiful prospect to a man shut
up in a dungeon.

As to shipping of its own, Ireland is so utterly
unprovided, that of all the excellent timber cut down
within these fifty or sixty years, it can hardly be said
that the nation has received the benefit of one valuable
house to dwell in, or one ship to trade with. Ireland
is the only kingdom I ever heard or read of, either in
ancient or modern story, which was denied the liberty
of exporting their native commodities and manufactures
wherever they pleased, except to countries at war with
their own prince or State : yet this privilege, by the
superiority of mere power, is refused us in the most

momentous parts of commerce; besides an act of navigation, to which we never consented, pinned down upon us, and rigorously executed; and a thousand other unexampled circumstances, as grievous as they are invidious to mention. To go on to the rest. It is too well known, that we are forced to obey some laws we never consented to; which is a condition I must not call by its true uncontroverted name, for fear of Lord Chief Justice Whitshed's ghost, with his *Libertas et natale solum* written for a motto on his coach, as it stood at the door of the court, while he was perjuring himself to betray both. Thus we are in the condition of patients, who have physic sent them by doctors at a distance, strangers to their constitution and the nature of their disease. . . .

As to the improvement of land, those few who attempt that or planting, through covetousness, or want of skill, generally leave things worse than they were; neither succeeding in trees nor hedges; and, by running into the fancy of grazing, after the manner of the Scythians, are every day depopulating the country.

We are so far from having a king to reside among us, that even the viceroy is generally absent four-fifths of his time in the government.

No strangers from other countries make this a part

of their travels ; where they can expect to see nothing but scenes of misery and desolation.

Those who have the misfortune to be born here, have the least title to any considerable employment ; to which they are seldom preferred, but upon a political consideration. One-third part of the rents of Ireland is spent in England ; which, with the profit of employments, pensions, appeals, journeys of pleasure or health, education at the Inns of Court and both Universities, remittances at pleasure, the pay of all superior officers in the army, and other incidents, will amount to a full half of the income of the whole kingdom, all clear profit to England.

We are denied the liberty of coining gold, silver, or even copper. In the Isle of Man they coin their own silver ; every petty prince, vassal to the Emperor, can coin what money he pleases. And in this, as in most of the articles already mentioned, we are an exception to all other states and monarchies that were ever known in the world.

As to the last, or fourteenth article, we take special care to act diametrically contrary to it in the whole course of our lives. Both sexes, but especially the women, despise and abhor to wear any of their own manufactures, even those which are better made than in other countries ; particularly a sort of silk plaid, through which the workmen are forced to run a kind of gold thread, that it may pass for Indian.

Even ale and potatoes are imported from England, as well as corn ; and our foreign trade is little more than importation of French wine, for which I am told we pay ready money.

Now, if all this be true (upon which I could easily enlarge), I should be glad to know, by what secret method it is that we grow a rich and flourishing people, without liberty, trade, manufactures, inhabitants, money, or the privilege of coining ; without industry, labour, or improvement of land ; and with more than half the rent and profits of the whole kingdom annually exported, for which we receive not a single farthing ; and to make up all this, nothing worth mentioning, except the linen of the North, a trade, casual, corrupted, and at mercy ; and some butter from Cork.   If we do flourish, it must be against every law of nature and reason ; like the thorn at Glastonbury, that blossoms in the midst of winter. . . .

There is not one argument used to prove the riches of Ireland, which is not a logical demonstration of its poverty.   The rise of our rents is squeezed out of the very blood, and vitals, and clothes, and dwellings of the tenants, who live worse than English beggars. The lowness of interest, in all other countries a sign of wealth, is in us a proof of misery; there being no trade to employ any borrower. Hence alone comes the dearness of land, since the savers have no other way to lay out their money; hence the dearness of necessaries of life; because the tenants cannot afford to pay such extravagant rates for land (which they must take, or go a'begging), without raising the price of cattle and of corn, although themselves should live upon chaff. Hence our increase of building in this city; because workmen have nothing to do but to employ one another, and one half of them are infallibly undone. Hence the daily increase of bankers, who may be a necessary evil in a trading country, but so ruinous in ours; who, for their private advantage, have sent away all our silver, and one-third of our gold; so that within three years past the running cash of the nation, which was about five hundred thousand pounds, is now less than two, and must daily diminish, unless we have liberty to coin, as well as that important kingdom the Isle of Man, and the meanest principality in the German empire, as I before observed.

I have sometimes thought, that this paradox of the kingdom's growing rich is chiefly owing to those worthy gentlemen the BANKERS ; who, except some custom-house officers, birds of passage, oppressive thrifty squires, and a few others who shall be nameless, are the only thriving among us : and I have often wished that a law were enacted to hang up half a dozen bankers every year, and thereby interpose at least some short delay to the farther ruin of Ireland.

Ye are idle ! ye are idle ! answered Pharaoh to the Israelites, when they complained to his Majesty that they were forced to make bricks without straw.

England enjoys every one of those advantages for enriching a nation which I have above enumerated ; and, into the bargain, a good million returned to them every year without labour or hazard, or one farthing value received on our side ; but how long we shall be able to continue the payment, I am not under the least concern. One thing I know, that, when the hen is starved to death, there will be no more golden eggs. I think it a little unhospitable, and others may call it a subtile piece of malice, that because there may be a dozen families in this town able to entertain their English friends in a generous manner at their tables, their guests upon their return to England shall report that we wallow in riches and luxury.

Yet I confess I have known an hospital, where all the

houschold officers grew rich ; while the poor, for whose sake it was built, were almost starved for want of food and raiment.

To conclude : If Ireland be a rich and flourishing kingdom, its wealth and prosperity must be owing to certain causes, that are yet concealed from the whole race of mankind ; and the effects are equally invisible. We need not wonder at strangers, when they deliver such paradoxes ; but a native and inhabitant of this kingdom, who gives the same verdict, must be either ignorant to stupidity, or a man-pleaser, at the expense of all honour, conscience, and truth.

THE STORY OF THE INJURED LADY.

*Written by herself, in a letter to her Friend;
with his answer.*

SIR,

Being ruined by the inconstancy and unkindness
of a lover, I hope a true and plain relation of my misfortunes may be of use and warning to credulous maids,
never to put too much trust in deceitful men.

A gentleman in the neighbourhood[1] had two mis-
tresses, another and myself;[2] and he pretended honourable love to us both. Our three houses stood pretty
near one another; his was parted from mine by a river,[3]
and from my rival's by an old broken wall.[4] But before
I enter into the particulars of this gentleman's hard
usage of me, I will give a very just and impartial character of my rival and myself.

As to her person, she is tall and lean, and very ill-

---

[1] England.
[2] Scotland and Ireland.
[3] The Irish Sea.
[4] The Pict's Wall.

shaped ; she has bad features, and a worse complexion.
As to her other qualities, she has no reputation either
for honesty, truth, or manners, and it is no wonder, considering what her education has been.   To sum up all,
she is poor and beggarly, and gets a sorry maintenance
by pilfering wherever she comes.

As for this gentleman, who is now so fond of her, she
still bears him an invincible hatred ; reviles him to his
face, and rails at him in all companies.   Her house is
frequented by a company of rogues and thieves, and
pickpockets, whom she encourages to rob his hen-roosts,
steal his corn and cattle, and do him all manner of mischief.[5]   She has been known to come at the head of
these rascals, and beat her lover until he was sore from
head to foot, and then force him to pay for the trouble
she was at.   Once, attended with a crew of ragamuffins,
she broke into his house, turned all things topsy-turvey,
and then set it on fire.   At the same time she told so
many lies among his servants that it set them all by the
ears, and his poor steward [6] was knocked on the head ;
for which I think, and so does all the country, that she
ought to be answerable.   To conclude her character:
she is of a different religion, being a Presbyterian of the

[5] An allusion to the border raids of the Highlanders.
[6] Charles I.

most rank and violent kind, and consequently having an inveterate hatred to the Church ; yet I am sure I have been always told, that in marriage there ought to be a union of minds as well as of persons.

I will now give my own character, and shall do it in few words, and with modesty and truth.   I was reckoned to be as handsome as any in our neighbour-hood, until I became pale and thin with grief and ill-usage.   I am still fair enough, and have, I think, no very ill features about me.   They that see me now will hardly allow me ever to have had any great·share of beauty ; for, besides being so much altered, I go always mobbed and in an undress, as well out of neglect, as indeed for want of clothes to appear in.   I might add to all this, that I was born to a good estate, although it now turns to little account under the oppressions I endure, and has been the true cause of all my misfortunes.

Some years ago, this gentleman, taking a fancy either to my person or fortune, made his addresses to me : which, being then young and foolish, I too readily ad-mitted.   When he had once got possession, he began to play the usual part of a too fortunate lover, affecting on all occasions to show his authority, and to act like a conqueror.   First, he found fault with the government of my family, which, I grant was none of the best, con-

sisting of ignorant, illiterate creatures, for at that time
I knew but little of the world.   In compliance to him,
therefore, I agreed to fall into his ways and methods
of living ; I consented that his steward should govern
my house, and have liberty to employ an under-
steward,[7] who should receive his directions. My lover
proceeded farther, turned away several old servants
and tenants, and supplying me with others from his own
house.   These grew so domineering and unreasonable,
that there was no quiet, and I heard of nothing but
perpetual quarrels, which, although I could not possibly help, yet my lover laid all the blame and punishment upon me ; and upon every falling out still turned
away more of my people, and supplied me in their stead
with a number of fellows and dependents of his own,
whom he had no other way to provide for. Over-
come by love, and to avoid noise and contention, I
yielded to all his usurpations, and finding it in vain
to resist, I thought it my best policy to make my
court to my new servants, and draw them to my
interests ; I fed them from my own table with the
best I had, put my new tenants on the choice parts of
my land, and treated them all so kindly that they
began to love me as well as their master.   In process

[7] The Lord-Lieutenant.

N

of time, all my old servants were gone, and I had not
a creature about me, nor above one or two tenants,
but what were of his choosing ; yet I had the good
luck, by gentle usage, to bring over the greatest part
of them to my side.   When my lover observed this, he
began to alter his language ; and to those who inquired
about me, he would answer that I was an old dependent
. upon his family, whom he had placed on some concerns
of his own ; and he began to use me accordingly, neg-
lecting, by degrees, all common civility in his behaviour.
I shall never forget the speech he made me one morning, which he delivered with all the gravity in the world.
He put me in mind of the vast obligations I lay under
to him in sending me so many of his people for my own
good, and to teach me manners : that it had cost him ten
times more than I was worth to maintain me ; that it
had been much better for him if I had been burnt, or
sunk to the bottom of the sea ; that it was reasonable I
should strain myself as far as I was able to reimburse
him some of his charges ; that from henceforward
he expected his word should be a law to me in all
things ; that I must maintain a parish-watch against
thieves and robbers, and give salaries to an overseer,
a constable, and others, all of his own choosing
whom he would send from time to time to be spies upon

me ; that, to enable me the better in supporting these
expenses, my tenants should be obliged to carry all
their goods across the river to his own town-market,
and pay toll on both sides, and then sell them at half
value.   But because we were a nasty sort of people, and
that he could not endure to touch anything that we had
a hand in, and, likewise, because he wanted work to
employ his own folks, therefore we must send all our
goods to his market just in their naturals—the milk immediately from the cow, without making into cheese or
butter ; the corn in the ear ; the grass as it was mowed ;
the wool as it comes from the sheep's back ; and bring
the fruit upon the branch, that he might not be obliged
to eat it after our filthy hands : that if a tenant carried
but a piece of bread and cheese to eat by the way, or an
inch of worsted to mend his stockings, he should forfeit
his whole parcel : and because a parcel of rogues usually
plied on the river between us, who often robbed my
tenants of their goods and boats, he ordered a water-
man of his to guard them, whose manner was to be out
of the way till the poor wretches were plundered, then
to overtake the thieves, and seize all as lawful prize to
his master and himself.   It would be endless to repeat a
hundred other hardships he has put upon me ; but it is
a general rule, that whenever he imagines the smallest

advantage will redound to one of his footboys by any new oppression of me and my whole family and estate, he never disputeth it a moment. All this has rendered me so very insignificant and contemptible at home, that some servants, to whom I pay the greatest wages, and many tenants, who have the most beneficial leases, are gone over to live with him, yet I am bound to continue their wages and pay their rents; by which means one-third of my income is spent on his estate, and above another third by his tolls and markets: and my poor tenants are so sunk and impoverished, that instead of maintaining me suitably to my quality, they can hardly find me clothes to keep me warm, or provide the common necessaries of life for themselves.

Matters being in this posture between me and my lover, I received intelligence that he had been for some time making very pressing overtures of marriage to my rival, until there happened to be some misunderstand-ings between them. She gave him ill words, and threatened to break off all commerce with him. He, on the other side, having either acquired courage by his triumphs over me, or supposing her to be as tame a fool as I, thought at first to carry it with a high hand, but hearing at the same time that she had thought of making some private proposals to join with me against him, and doubting, with very good reason, that I would readily accept them, he seemed very much disconcerted.[8] This, I thought, was a proper occasion to show some great example of generosity and love ; and so, without farther consideration, I sent him word, that hearing there was likely to be a quarrel betwixt him and my rival, notwithstanding all that had passed, and without binding him to any conditions in my own favour, I would stand by him against her and all the world, while I had a penny in my purse, or a petticoat to pawn. This message was subscribed by all my chief tenants, and proved so powerful, that my rival immediately grew more tractable upon it. The result of which was, that there is now a treaty of marriage concluded between them,[9] the wedding clothes are bought, and nothing remains but to perform the ceremony, which is put off for some days, because they design it to be a public wedding. And to reward my love, constancy, and generosity, he has bestowed on me the office of being sempstress to his grooms and footmen, which I am forced to accept or starve.[1] Yet, in the midst of this my situation, I cannot but have some pity for this deluded man.

[8] An allusion to the strained relations between England and Scotland, caused by the passing of the Scottish Act of Security.
[9] The Union.
[1] An allusion to the Irish linen trade.

For my part, I think, and so does all the country, too, that the man is possessed ; at least none of us are able to imagine what he can possibly see in her, unless she has bewitched him, or given him some powder.

I am sure I never sought this alliance, and you can bear me witness that I might have had other matches ; nay if I were lightly disposed, I could still perhaps have offers, that some, who hold their heads higher, would be glad to accept. But alas ! I never had any such wicked thought ; all I now desire is, only to enjoy a little quiet, to be free from the persecutions of this unreasonable man, and that he will let me manage my own little fortune to the best advantage ; for which I will undertake to pay him a considerable pension every year, much more considerable than what he now gets by his oppressions ; for he must needs find himself a loser at last, when he has drained me and my tenants so dry, that we shall not have a penny for him or ourselves. There is one imposition of his I had almost forgot, which I think unsufferable, and will appeal to you, or any reasonable person, whether it be so or not. I told you before, that by an old compact we agreed to have the same steward ; at which time I consented likewise to regulate my family and estate by the same method with him, which he then showed me written down in form, and I approved of. Now, the turn he thinks fit to give this compact of ours is very extraordinary ; for he pretends, that whatever orders he shall think fit to prescribe for the future in his family, he may, if he will, compel mine to observe them without asking my advice, or hearing my reasons.

So that I must not make a lease without his consent, or give any directions for the well-governing of my family, but what he countermands whenever he pleases. This leaves me at such confusion and uncertainty, that my servants know not when to obey me ; and my tenants, although many of them be very well-inclined, seem quite at a loss.

But I am too tedious upon this melancholy subject, which however I hope you will forgive, since the happiness of my whole life depends upon it. I desire you will think awhile, and give your best advice what measures I shall take with prudence, justice, courage, and honour, to protect my liberty and fortune against the hardships and severities I lie under from that unkind, inconstant man.

THE ANSWER TO THE INJURED LADY.

MADAM,

I have received your ladyship's letter, and carefully considered every part of it, and shall give you my opinion how you ought to proceed for your own security. But first I must beg leave to tell your ladyship, that you were guilty of an unpardonable weakness the other day, in making that offer to your lover of standing by him in any quarrel he might have with your rival. You know very well, that she began to apprehend he had designs of using her as he had done you; and common prudence might have directed you rather to have entered into some measures with her for joining against him, until he might at least be brought to some reasonable terms; but your invincible hatred to that lady has carried your resentments so high, as to be the cause of your ruin; yet if you please to consider, this aversion of yours began a good while before she became your rival, and was taken up by you and your family in a sort of com-

pliment to your lover, who formerly had a great abhor-
rence of her.   It is true, since that time you have
suffered very much by her encroachments upon your
estate,[1] but she never pretended to govern and direct
you ; and now you have drawn a new enemy upon
yourself; for I think you may count upon all the ill
offices she can possibly do you, by her credit with her
husband ; whereas, if, instead of openly declaring against
her, without any provocation, you had but sat still
awhile, and said nothing, that gentleman would have
lessened his severity to you out of perfect fear.   This
weakness of yours you call generosity ; but I doubt
there was more in the matter: in short, madam, I
have good reasons to think you were betrayed to it by
the pernicious counsel of some about you ; for to
my certain knowledge, several of your tenants and
servants to whom you have been very kind, are as
arrant rascals as any in the country. I know the
matters of fact, as you relate them, are true, and fairly
represented.

My advice therefore is this : get your tenants together
as   soon as you conveniently can, and make them
agree to the following resolutions.

First, that your family and servants have no depend-

---

[1] An allusion to the Scotch Colonists in Ulster.

ence upon the said gentleman, farther than by the old agreement, which obliges you to have the same steward, and to regulate your household by such methods as you should both agree to.

Secondly, that you will not carry your goods to the market of his town, unless you please, nor be hindered from carrying them anywhere else.

Thirdly, that the servants you pay wages to shall live at home, or forfeit their places.

Fourthly, that whatever lease you make to a tenant, it shall not be in his power to break it.

If he will agree to these articles, I advise you to contribute as largely as you can to all charges of parish and county.

I can assure you, several of that gentleman's ablest tenants and servants are against his severe usage of you and would be glad of an occasion to convince the rest of their error, if you will not be wanting to yourself.

If the gentleman refuses these just and reasonable offers, pray let me know it, and perhaps I may think of something else that will be more effectual.

I am,

Madam,

Your Ladyship's, etc.

A LETTER TO THE ARCHBISHOP OF DUBLIN,[1] CONCERNING THE WEAVERS.

MY LORD,

The corporation of weavers in the woollen manu-facture, who have so often attended your Grace, and called upon me with their schemes and proposals, were with me on Thursday last; when he who spoke for the rest, and in the name of his absent brethren, said, " It was the opinion of the whole body, that if somewhat was written at this time, by an able hand, to persuade the people of this kingdom to wear their own woollen manufactures, it might be of good use to the nation in general, and preserve many hundreds of their trade from starving."

To which I answered, " That it was hard for any man of common spirit to turn his thoughts to such specu-lations, without discovering a resentment, which people are too delicate to bear." For I will not deny to your Grace, that I cannot reflect on the singular condition of

[1] Dr. William King, the friend and correspondent of Swift.

this country, different from all others upon the face of
the earth, without some emotion; and without often
examining, as I pass the streets, whether those animals
which come in my way, with two legs and human faces,
clad and erect, be of the same species with what I have
seen very like them in England as to the outward shape,
but differing in their notions, natures, and intellectuals,
more than any two kinds of brutes in the forest; which
any man of common prudence would immediately discover, by persuading them to define what they meant
by law, liberty, property, courage, reason, loyalty, or
religion.

One thing, my lord, I am very confident of; that if
God Almighty, for our sins, would most justly send us a
pestilence, whoever should dare to discover his grief in
public for such a visitation, would certainly be censured for disaffection to the government; for I solemnly
profess that I do not know one calamity we have under-
gone these many years, which any man, whose opinions
were not in fashion, dared to lament, without being
openly charged with that imputation.   And this is the
harder, because although a mother, when she has cor-
rected her child, may sometimes force it to kiss the rod.
yet she will never give that power to the footboy or
the scullion.

My lord, there are two things for the people of this kingdom to consider; first, their present evil condition; and secondly, what can be done in some degree to remedy it. . . . I am weary of so many abortive projects for the advancement of trade; of so many crude proposals, in letters sent me from unknown hands; of so many contradictory speculations, about raising or sinking the value of gold and silver. I am not in the least sorry to hear of the great numbers going to America, although very much for the causes that drive them from us, since the uncontrouled maxim, "That people are the riches of a nation," is no maxim here under our circumstances. We have neither manufactures to employ them about, nor food to support them. If a private gentleman's income be sunk irretrievably for ever, from a hundred pounds to fifty, and he has no other method to supply the deficiency; I desire to know, my lord, whether such a person has any other course to take, than to sink half his expenses in every article of economy, to save himself from ruin and a gaol.

Is not this more than doubly the case of Ireland, where the want of money, the irretrievable ruin of trade, with the other evils above-mentioned, and many more too well known and felt, and too numerous or invidious to be related, have been gradually sinking us, for above a dozen years past, to a degree, that we are at least by two-thirds in a worse condition than was ever known since the Revolution ? Therefore, instead of dreams and projects for the advancing of trade, we have nothing left but to find out some expedient, whereby we may reduce our expenses to our incomes.

Yet this procedure, allowed so necessary in all private families, and in its own nature so easy to put in practice, may meet with strong opposition by the cowardly slavish indulgence of the men, to the intolerable pride, arrogance, vanity, and luxury of the women ; who, strictly adhering to the rules of modern education, seem to employ their whole stock of invention in contriving new arts of profusion, faster than the most parsimonious husband can afford : and, to compass this work the more effectually, their universal maxim is, to despise and detest everything of the growth of their own country, and most to value whatever comes from the very remotest parts of the globe. And I am convinced that if the virtuosi could once find out a world in the moon, with a passage to it, our women would wear nothing but what directly came from thence. The prime cost of wine yearly imported to Ireland is valued at thirty thousand pounds ; and the tea (including coffee and chocolate) at five times that sum. The laces, silks, calicoes, and all other unnecessary ornaments for women, including English cloths and stuffs, added to the former articles, make up (to compute grossly) about four hundred thousand pounds.   Now if we should allow the thirty thousand pounds, wherein the women have their share, and which is all we have to comfort us, and deduct seventy thousand pounds more for over-reaching, there would still remain three hundred thousand pounds, annually spent, for unwholesome drugs and unnecessary finery ; which prodigious sum would be wholly saved, and many thousands of our miserable shopkeepers and manufacturers comfortably supported.

Let speculative people bury their brains as they please, there is no other way to prevent this kingdom from sinking for ever, than by utterly renouncing all foreign dress and luxury.

It is absolutely so in fact, that every husband of any fortune in the kingdom, is nourishing a poisonous, devouring serpent in his bosom, with all the mischief, but with none of its wisdom.

If all the women were clad with the growth of their own country, they might still vie with each other in the course of foppery ; and still have room left to vie with each other and equally show their wit and judgment, in deciding upon the variety of Irish stuffs.   And if they could be contented with their native wholesome slops for breakfast, we should hear no more of the spleen, hysterics, colics, palpitations, and asthmas. They might still be allowed to ruin each other and their husbands at play, because the money lost would circulate among ourselves.

My lord, I freely own it a wild imagination, that any words will cure the sottishness of men, or the vanity of women; but the kingdom is in a fair way of producing the most effectual remedy, when there will not be money left for the common course of buying and selling the very necessaries of life in our markets, unless we absolutely change the whole method of our proceedings.

The corporation of weavers in woollen and silk, who have so frequently offered proposals both to your Grace and to me, are the hottest and coldest generation of men that I have known. About a month ago, they attended your Grace, when I had the honour to be with you; and designed me the same favour. They desired you would recommend to your clergy to wear gowns of Irish stuffs which might probably spread the example among all their brethren in the kingdom; and perhaps among the lawyers and gentlemen of the university, and among the citizens of those corporations who appear in gowns on solemn occasions. I then mentioned a kind of stuff, not above eightpence a yard, which I heard had been

contrived by some of the trade, and was very convenient. I desired they would prepare some of that, or
any sort of black stuff, on a certain day, when your
Grace would appoint as many clergymen as could readily
be·found to meet at your palace ; and there give their
opinions ; and that your Grace's visitation approaching,
you could then have the best opportunity of seeing what
could be done in a matter of such consequence, as they
seemed to think, to the woollen manufacture. But
instead of attending, as was expected, they came to me
a fortnight after with a new proposal, that something
should be written by an acceptable and able hand, to
promote in general the wearing of home manufactures ;
and their civilities would fix that work upon me.

I asked if they had prepared the stuffs, as they had
promised, and your Grace expected ; but they had not
made the least step in the matter, nor, as it appears,
thought of it more.

I did, some years ago, propose to the masters and
principal dealers in the home-manufactures of silk and
wool, that they should meet together ; and, after mature
consideration, publish advertisements to the following
purpose :—

"That in order to encourage the wearing of Irish
manufactures in silk and woollen, they gave notice to

O

the nobility and gentry of the kingdom, that they, the undersigned, would enter into bonds, for themselves and for e ch other, to sell the several sorts of stuffs, cloths, and silks, made to the best perfection they were able, for certain fixed prices ; and in such a manner, that if a child were sent to any of their shops, the buyer might be secure of the value and goodness and measure of the ware ; and, lest this might be thought to look like a monopoly, any other member of the trade might be admitted, upon such conditions as should be agreed on. And if any person whatsoever should complain that he was ill-used, in the value and goodness of what he bought, the matter should be examined, the persons injured be fully satisfied by the whole corporation without delay, and the dishonest seller be struck out of the society, unless it appeared evidently that the failure proceeded only from mistake."

The mortal danger is, that if these dealers could prevail, by the goodness and cheapness of their cloths and stuffs, to give a turn to the principal people of Ireland in favour of their goods ; they would relapse into the knavish practice, peculiar to this kingdom, which is apt to run through all trades, even so low as a common aleseller ; who, as soon as he gets a vogue for his liquor, and outsells his neighbours, thinks his credit will put

off the worst he can buy till his customers will come no
more. Thus, I have known at London, in a general
mourning, the drapers dye black all their damaged
goods, and sell them at double rates ; then complain,
and petition the Court, that they are ready to starve
by the continuance of the mourning.

Therefore, I say, those principal weavers who would
enter into such a compact as I have mentioned, must
give sufficient security against all such practices ; for if
once the women can persuade their husbands that
foreign goods, besides the finery, will be as cheap, and do
more service, our last state will be worse than the first.

I do not here pretend to digest perfectly the method
by which these principal shop-keepers shall proceed, in
such a proposal ; but my meaning is clear enough, and
cannot be reasonably objected against.

We have seen what a destructive loss the kingdom
received by the detestable fraud of the merchants, or
northern linen weavers, or both ; notwithstanding all
the cares of the governor of that board, when we had
an offer of commerce with the Spaniards for our linens
to the value, as I am told, of thirty thousand pounds a
year. But, while we deal like pedlars, we shall practise
like pedlars, and sacrifice all honesty to the present
urging advantage.

What I have said may serve as an answer to the desire made me by the corporation of weavers, that I would offer my notions to the public. As to anything farther, let them apply themselves to the Parliament in their next session. Let them prevail on the House of Commons to grant one very reasonable request ; and I shall think there is still some spirit left in the nation, when I read a vote to this purpose : " Resolved, *nemine contradicente*, That this House will, for the future, wear no clothes but such as are made of Irish growth, or of Irish manufacture, nor will permit their wives or children to wear any other ; and that they will, to the utmost, endeavour to prevail with their friends, relations, dependents, and tenants, to follow their example." And if, at the same time, they could banish tea and coffee, and china-ware, out of their families, and force their wives to chat their scandal over an infusion of sage, or other wholesome domestic vegetables, we might possibly be able to subsist, and pay our absentees, pensioners, generals, civil officers, appeals, colliers, temporary travellers, students, school-boys, splenetic visitors of Bath, Tunbridge, and Epsom, with all other smaller drains, by sending our crude, unwrought goods to England, and receiving from thence, and all other countries, nothing but what is fully manufactured, and

keep a few potatoes and 'oatmeal for our own sub
sistence.

I have been for a dozen years past wisely prognosti-
cating the present condition of this kingdom ; which
any human creature of common sense could foretell,
with as little sagacity as myself.   My meaning is, that
a consumptive body must needs die, which has spent
all its spirits, and received no nourishment.   Yet I am
often tempted to pity, when I hear the poor farmer and
cottager lamenting the hardness of the times, and im-
puting them either to one or two ill seasons, which
better climates than ours are more exposed to ; or to
scarcity of silver, which, to a nation of liberty, would
only be a slight and temporary inconvenience, to be
removed at a month's warning.

TWO LETTERS ON SUBJECTS RELATIVE TO THE IMPROVEMENT OF IRELAND.

I.

TO MESSRS. TRUMAN AND LAYFIELD.

GENTLEMEN,—

I am inclined to think that I received a letter from you two, last summer, directed to Dublin, while I was in the country, whither it was sent me ; and I ordered an answer to it to be printed, but it seems it had little effect, and I suppose this will not have much more. But the heart of this people is waxed gross, and their ears are dull of hearing, and their eyes they have closed. And, gentlemen, I am to tell you another thing : that the world is too regardless of what we write for public good ; that after we have delivered our thoughts, without any prospect of advantage, or of reputation, which latter is not to be had but by subscribing our names, we cannot prevail upon a printer to be at the charge of sending it into the world unless we will be at all or half the expense ; and although we are willing enough to bestow our labours, we think it unreasonable to be out of pocket ; because it probably may not consist with the situation of our affairs.

I do very much approve your good intentions, and in a great measure your manner of declaring them ; and I do imagine you intended that the world should not only know your sentiments, but my answer, which I shall impartially give. . . . Although your letter be directed to me, yet I take myself to be only an imaginary person ; for, although I conjecture I had formerly one from you, yet I never answered it otherwise than in print ; neither was I at a loss to know the reasons why so many people of this kingdom were transporting themselves to America.

And if this encouragement were owing to a pamphlet written, giving an account of the country of Pennsylvania, to tempt people to go thither, I do declare that those who were tempted, by such a narrative, to such a journey, were fools, and the author a most impudent knave ; at least, if it be the same pamphlet I saw when it first came out, which is about twenty-five years ago, dedicated to William Penn (whom by a mistake you call "Sir William Penn,") and styling him,

by authority of the Scripture, "Most noble Governor."
For I was very well acquainted with Penn, and did,
some years after, talk with him upon that pamphlet,
and the impudence of the author, who spoke so many
things in praise of the soil and climate, which Penn
himself did absolutely contradict. For he did assure
me, "That this country wanted the shelter of mountains, which left it open to the northern winds from
Hudson's Bay and the Frozen Sea, which destroyed all
plantations of trees, and was even pernicious to all common vegetables." But, indeed, New York, Virginia,
and other parts less northward, or more defended by
mountains, are described as excellent countries ; but
upon what conditions of advantage foreigners go
thither, I am yet to seek. What evils our people avoid
by running from hence, is easier to be determined.
They conceive themselves to live under the tyranny of
most cruel exacting landlords, who have no views
farther than increasing their rent-rolls. Secondly, you
complain of the want of trade, whereof you seem not
to know the reason. Thirdly, you lament most justly
the money spent by absentees in England. Fourthly,
you complain that your linen manufacture declines.
Fifthly, that your tithe collectors oppress you. Sixthly,
that your children have no hopes of preferment in the

church, the revenue, or the army; to which you might have added the law, and all civil employments whatsoever. Seventhly, you are undone for want of silver, and want all other money.

I could easily add some other motives, which, to men of spirit, who desire and expect, and think they deserve the common privileges of human nature, would be of more force, than any you have yet named, to drive them out of this kingdom. But as these speculations may probably not much affect the brains of your people, I shall choose to let them pass unmentioned. . . . I must confess to you both, that if one reason of your people's deserting us be the despair of things growing better in their own country, I have not one syllable to answer; because that would be to hope for what is impossible, and so I have been telling the public these ten years. For there are events which must precede any such blessing; first, a liberty of trade; secondly, a share of preferments in all kinds, equal to the British natives; and thirdly, a return of those absentees, who take almost one half of the kingdom's revenue. As to the first and second, there is nothing left us but despair; and for the third, it will never happen till the kingdom has no money to send them; for which, in my own particular, I shall not be sorry. The exactions of landlords has indeed been a grievance of above twenty years' standing. But as to what you object about the severe clauses relating to the improvement, the fault lies wholly on the other side ; for the landlords, either by their igno- rance, or greediness of making large rent-rolls, have performed this matter so ill, as we see by experience, that there is not one tenant in five hundred who has made any improvement worth mentioning : for which I appeal to any man who rides through the kingdom, where little is to be found among the tenants but beggary and desolation; the cabins of the Scotch themselves, in Ulster, being as dirty and miserable as those of the wildest Irish. Whereas good firm penal laws for im- provement, with a tolerable easy rent, and a reasonable period of time, would, in twenty years, have increased the rents of Ireland at least a third part of the intrinsic value. I am glad to hear you speak with some decency of the clergy, and to impute the exactions you lament to the managers or farmers of the tithes. But you entirely mistake the fact ; for I defy the most wicked and most powerful clergyman in the kingdom to oppress the meanest farmer in the parish ; and I defy the same clergyman to prevent himself from being cheated by the same farmer, whenever that farmer shall be disposed to be knavish or peevish.

For, although the Ulster tithing-teller is more advantageous to the clergy than any other in the kingdom, yet the minister can demand no more than his tenth ; and where the corn much exceeds the small tithes, as, except in some districts, I am told it always does, he is at the mercy of every stubborn farmer, especially of those whose sect as well as interest incline them to opposition. However, I take it that your people bent for America do not show the best side of their prudence in making this one part of their complaint ; yet they are so far wise, as not to make the payment of tithes a scruple of ·conscience, which is too gross for any Protestant dissenter, except a Quaker, to pretend. But do your people indeed think, that if tithes were abolished, or delivered into the hands of the landlord, after the blessed manner in the Scotch spiritual economy, the tenant would sit easier in his rent under the same person, who must be lord of the soil and of the tithe together ?

I am ready enough to grant, that the oppression of landlords, the utter ruin of trade, with its necessary consequences, the want of money, half the revenues of the kingdom spent abroad, the continued dearth of three years, and the strong delusion in your people by false allurement from America, may be the chief motives of their eagerness after such an expedition. But there is likewise another temptation, which is not of inconsiderable weight ; which is their itch of living in a country where their sect is predominant, and where their eyes and consciences will not be offended by the stumbling-block of ceremonies, habits, and spiritual titles. But I was surprised to find that those calamities, whereof we are innocent, have been sufficient to drive many families out of their country, who had no reason to complain of oppressive landlords.   For, while I was last year in the northern parts, a person of quality, whose estate was let above twenty years ago, and then at a very reasonable rent, some for leases of lives, and some perpetuities, did, in a few months, purchase eleven of those leases at a very inconsiderable price, although they were, two years ago, reckoned to pay but half value ; whence it is manifest that our present miserable condition, and the dismal prospect of worse, with other reasons above assigned, are sufficient to put men upon trying this desperate experiment of changing the scene they are in, although landlords should, by a miracle, become less inhuman.

There is hardly a scheme proposed for improving the trade of this kingdom, which does not manifestly show the stupidity and ignorance of the proposer, and I laugh

with contempt at those weak wise heads, who proceed
upon general maxims, or advise us to follow the examples
of Holland and England.   These empirics talk by rote,
without understanding the constitution of the kingdom :
as if a physician, knowing that exercise contributed
much to health, should prescribe to his patient under
a severe fit of the gout, to walk ten miles every morning.   The directions for Ireland are very short and
plain : to encourage agriculture and home consumption,
and. utterly discard all importations which are not
absolutely necessary for health or life.   And how few
necessaries, conveniences, or even comforts of life, are
denied us by nature, or not to be attained by labour and
industry !   Are those detestable extravagances of
Flanders lace, English cloths made of our own wool, and
other goods, Italian or Indian silks, tea, coffee, chocolate,
china-ware, and that profusion of wines, by the knavery
of merchants growing dearer every season, with a
hundred unnecessary fopperies, better known to others
than me, are these, I say, fit for us, any more than for the
beggar who could not eat his veal without oranges ?

Is it not the highest indignity to human nature, that
men should be such poltroons as to suffer the kingdom
and themselves to be undone by the vanity, the folly,
the pride, and wantonness of their wives, who, under

their present corruptions, seem to be a kind of animal, suffered, for our sins, to be sent into the world for the destruction of families, societies, and kingdoms, and whose whole study seems directed to be as expensive as they possibly can, in every useless article of living ; who, by long practice, can reconcile the most pernicious foreign drugs to their health and pleasure, provided they are but expensive, as starlings grow fat with henbane ; who contract a robustness by mere practice of sloth and luxury ; who can play deep several hours after mid-night, sleep beyond noon, revel upon Indian poisons, and spend the revenues of a moderate family to adorn a nauseous, unwholesome, living carcase ?   Let those few who are not concerned in any part of this accusa-tion, suppose it unsaid ; let the rest take it among them. Gracious God, in His mercy, look down upon a nation so shamefully besotted ! . . .

Is there any mortal who can show me, under the circumstances we stand with our neighbours, under their inclinations towards us, under laws never to be repealed, under the desolation caused by absentees, under many other circumstances not to be mentioned, that this kingdom can ever be a nation of trade, or subsist by any other method than that of a reduced family, by the utmost parsimony ? . . .

ANSWER TO SEVERAL LETTERS SENT FROM
UNKNOWN HANDS. 1729.

I AM very well pleased with the good opinion you express of me, and wish it were any way in my power to
answer your expectations, for the service of my country.
I have carefully read your several schemes and proposals,
which you think should be offered to Parliament. In
answer, I will assure you, that, in another place, I have
known very good proposals rejected with contempt by
public assemblies, merely because they were offered from
without doors, and yours, perhaps, might have the same
fate, especially if handed to the public by me, who am
not acquainted with three members, nor have the least
interest with one. My printers have been twice prosecuted, to my great expense, on account of discourses I
writ for the public service, without the least reflection
on parties or persons, and the success I had in those of
the Drapier, was not owing to my abilities, but to a
lucky juncture, when the fuel was ready for the first
hand that would be at the pains of kindling it. It is
true, both those envenomed prosecutions were the workmanship of a judge, who is now gone *to his own place.*

But, let that be as it will, I am determined, henceforth never to be the instrument of leaving an innocent man at the mercy of that bench. It is certain there are several particulars relating to this kingdom (I have mentioned a few of them in one of my Drapier's letters), which it were heartily to be wished that the Parliament would take under their consideration, such as will no way interfere with England, otherwise than to its advantage.

The first I shall mention, is touched at in a letter which I received from one of you, gentlemen, about the highways; which, indeed, are almost everywhere scandalously neglected. I know a very rich man in this city, a true lover and saver of his money, who, being possessed of some adjacent lands, has been at great charge in repairing effectually the roads that lead to them, and, has assured me that his lands are thereby advanced four or five shillings an acre, by which he gets treble interest. But, generally speaking, all over the kingdom the roads are deplorable, and, what is more particularly barbarous there is no sort of provision made for travellers on foot ; no, not near the city, except in a very few places, and in a most wretched manner : whereas the English are so particularly careful in this point, that you may travel there a hundred miles with less inconvenience than one

mile here.   But, since this may be thought too great a
reformation, I shall only speak of roads for horses,
carriages, and cattle.

Ireland is, I think, computed to be one-third smaller
than England ; yet, by some natural disadvantages, it
would not bear quite the same proportion in value, with
the same encouragement.   However, it has so happened,
for many years past, that it never arrived to above one-
eleventh part in point of riches, and of late, by the continual decrease of trade, and the increase of absentees,
with other circumstances not here to be mentioned,
hardly to a fifteenth part ; at least, if my calculations be
right, which I doubt are a little too favourable on our side.

Now, supposing day-labour to be cheaper by one half
here than in England, and our roads, by the nature of
our carriages, and the desolation of our country, to be
not worn and beaten above one-eighth part so much as
those of England, which is a very moderate computation,
I do not see why the mending of them would be a
greater burden to this kingdom than to that.

There have been, I believe, twenty Acts of Parliament,
in six or seven years of the late King, for mending long
tracts of impassable ways in several counties of England,
by erecting turnpikes, and receiving passage-money in a
manner that everybody knows.

P

If what I have advanced be true, it would be hard to give a reason against the same practice here ; since the necessity is as great, the advantage, in proportion, perhaps much greater, the materials of stone and gravel as easy to be found, and the workmanship, at least, twice as cheap.

Besides, the work may be done gradually, with allowances for the poverty of the nation, by so many perch a-year ; but with a special care to encourage skill and diligence, and to prevent fraud in the undertakers, to which we are too liable, and which are not always confined to those of the meaner sort ; but against these, no doubt, the wisdom of the nation may and will provide. Another evil, which, in my opinion, deserves the public care, is the ill management of the bogs; the neglect whereof is a much greater mischief to this kingdom than most people seem to be aware of.

It is allowed, indeed, by those who are esteemed most skilful in such matters, that the red, swelling mossy bog, whereof we have so many large tracts in this island, is not by any means to be fully reduced ; but the skirts, which are covered with a green coat, easily may, being not accretion, or annual growth of moss, like the other.

Now, the landlords are generally so careless as to

suffer their tenants to cut their turf in these skirts, as well as the bog adjoined ; whereby there is yearly lost a considerable quantity of land throughout the kingdom, never to be recovered.

But this is not the greatest part of the mischief ; for the main bog, although, perhaps, not reducible to natural soil, yet, by continuing large, deep, straight canals through the middle, cleaned at proper times as low as the channel or gravel, would become secure summer-pasture ; the margins might, with great profit and ornament, be filled with quickens, birch, and other trees proper for such a soil, and the canals be convenient for water-carriage of the turf, which is now drawn upon sled-cars, with great expense, difficulty, and loss of time, by reason of the many turf-pits scattered irregularly through the bog, wherein great numbers of cattle are yearly drowned.   And it has been, I confess, to me a matter of the greatest vexation, as well as wonder, to think how any landlord could be so absurd as suffer such havoc to be made.

All the acts for encouraging plantations of forest-trees are, I am told, extremely defective ; which, with great submission, must have been owing to a defect of skill in the contrivers of them.   In this climate, by the continual blowing of the west-south-west wind, hardly any tree of value will come to perfection that is not planted in groves, except very rarely, and where there is much land-shelter. I have not, indeed, read all the acts ; but, from inquiry, I cannot learn that the planting in groves is enjoined. And as to the effects of these laws, I have not seen the least, in many hundred miles' riding, except about a very few gentlemen's houses, and even those with very little skill or success. In all the rest, the hedges generally miscarry, as well as the larger, slender twigs planted upon the tops of ditches, merely for want of common skill and care.

I do not believe that a greater and quicker profit could be made, than by planting large groves of ash a few feet asunder, which in seven years would make the best kind of hop-poles, and grow in the same or less time to a second crop from their roots.

It would likewise be of great use and beauty in our desert scenes, to oblige cottagers to plant ash or elm before their cabins, and round their potato-gardens, where cattle either do not or ought not to come to destroy them.

The common objection against all this, drawn from the laziness, the perverseness, or thievish disposition of the poor native Irish, might be easily answered by show-ing the true reasons for such accusations, and how easily those people may be brought to a less savage manner of life ; but my printers have already suffered too much for my speculations.

However, supposing the size of a native's understanding just equal to that of a dog or a horse, I have often seen those two animals civilized by rewards, at least as much as by punishments.

It would be a noble achievement to abolish the Irish language in this kingdom, so far at least as to oblige all the natives to speak only English on every occasion of business, in shops, markets, fairs, and other places of dealing : yet I am wholly deceived, if this might not be effectually done in less than half an age, and at a very trifling expense ; for such I look upon a tax to be of only six thousand pounds a-year, to accomplish so great a work. This would, in a great measure, civilize the most barbarous among them, reconcile them to our customs and manner of living, and reduce great numbers to the national religion, whatever kind may then happen to be established.

This method is plain and simple ; and although I am too desponding to produce it, yet I could heartily wish some public thoughts were employed to reduce this uncultivated people from that idle, savage, beastly, thievish manner of life, in which they continue sunk to such a degree, that it is almost impossible for a country gentleman to find a servant of human capacity, or the least tincture of natural honesty, or who does not live among his own tenants in continual fear of having his plantations destroyed, his cattle stolen, and his goods pilfered.

The love, affection, or vanity of living in England, continuing to carry thither so many wealthy families, the consequences thereof, together with the utter loss of all trade, except what is detrimental, which has forced such great numbers of weavers, and others, to seek their bread in foreign countries ; the unhappy practice of stocking such vast quantities of land with sheep and other cattle, which reduces twenty families to one ; those events, I say, have exceedingly depopulated this kingdom for several years past. I should heartily wish therefore, under this miserable dearth of money, that those who are most concerned would think it advisable to save a hundred thousand pounds a year, which is now sent out of this kingdom, to feed us with corn. There is not an older or more uncontroverted maxim in the politics of all wise nations, than that of encouraging agriculture ; and therefore, to what kind of wisdom a practice so directly contrary among us may be reduced I am by no means a judge. If labour and people make the true riches of a nation, what must be the issue where one part of the people are forced away, and the other have nothing to do ?

If it should be thought proper by wiser heads, that his Majesty might be applied to in a national way, for giving the kingdom leave to coin halfpence for its own use, I believe no good subject will be under the least apprehension that such a request could meet with refusal, or the least delay. Perhaps we are the only kingdom upon earth, or that ever was or will be upon earth, which did not enjoy that common right of civil society, under the proper inspection of its prince or legislature, to coin money of all usual metals for its own occasions. Every petty prince in Germany, vassal to the Emperor, enjoys this privilege. And I have seen in this kingdom several silver pieces, with the inscription of CIVITAS WATERFORD, DROGHEDAGH, and other towns.

THE PRESENT MISERABLE STATE OF IRELAND.

THIS letter was addressed to Sir Robert Walpole on Swift's return to Ireland in 1726 before his final rupture with the Premier the following year. Swift endeavoured to combat the English prejudices of the minister on the mode of managing Ireland, seeking the emancipation of his country rather than personal advancement. Here he seems to assume the character of the Drapier besides adding his initials.

SIR,

By the last packets I had the favour of yours, and am surprised that you should apply to a person so ill-qualified as I am, for a full and impartial account of the state of our trade. I have always lived as retired as possible; I have carefully avoided the perplexed honour of city-offices; I have never minded anybody's business but my own; upon all which accounts, and

several others, you might easily have found among my
fellow-citizens, persons more capable to resolve the
weighty questions you put to me than I can pretend to
be. But being entirely at leisure, even at this season of
the year, when I used to have scarce time sufficient to
perform the necessary offices of life, I will endeavour to
comply with your requests, cautioning you not implicitly
to rely upon what I say, excepting what belongs to that
branch of trade in which I am more immediately concerned.

The Irish trade is, at present, in the most deplorable
condition that can be imagined ; to remedy it, the causes
of its languishment must be inquired into. But as
those causes (you may assure yourself) will not be
removed, you may look upon it as a thing past hope of
recovery.

The first and greatest shock our trade received was
from an act passed in the reign of King William, in the
Parliament of England, prohibiting the exportation of
wool manufactured in Ireland, an act (as the event
plainly shows) fuller of greediness than good policy ; an
act as beneficial to France and Spain, as it has been
destructive to England and Ireland. At the passing of
this fatal act, the condition of our trade was glorious and
flourishing, though no way interfering with the English ;

we made no broadcloths above 6s. per yard; coarse druggets, bays and shalloons, worsted damasks, strong draught-works, slight half-works, and gaudy stuffs, were the only products of our looms : these were partly consumed by the meanest of our people, and partly sent to the northern nations, from which we had in exchange timber, iron, hemp, flax, pitch, tar, and hard dollars. At the time the current money of Ireland was foreign silver, a man could hardly receive 100*l*., without finding the coin of all the northern powers, and every prince of the empire among it.

This money was returned into England for fine cloths silks, &c., for our own wear, for rent, for coals, for hardware, and all other English manufactures, and in a great measure supplied the London merchants with foreign silver for exportation.

The repeated clamours of the English weavers produced this act, so destructive to themselves and us.

They looked with envious eyes upon our prosperity, and complained of being undersold by us in those commodities which themselves did not deal in. At their instances the act was passed, and we lost our profitable northern trade. Have they got it? No; surely you have found out they have ever since declined in the trade they so happily possessed? You shall find (if I am rightly

informed) towns without one loom in them, which sub-
sisted entirely upon the woollen manufactory before the
passing of this unhappy bill; and I will try if I can
give the true reasons for the decay of their trade, and
our calamities.

Three parts in four of the inhabitants of that dis-
trict of the town where I dwell were English manufacturers, whom either misfortunes in trade, little petty
debts contracted through idleness, or the pressures of
a numerous family, had driven into our cheap country. These were employed in working up our coarse
wool, while the finest was sent into England. Several
of these had taken the children of the native Irish
apprentices to them, who being humbled by the for-
feiture of upward of three millions by the Revolution,
were obliged to stoop to a mechanic industry. Upon
the passing of this bill, we were obliged to dismiss
thousands of these people from our service. Those
who had settled their affairs returned home, and overstocked England with workmen; those whose debts
were unsatisfied went to France, Spain, and the
Netherlands, where they met with good encouragement, whereby the natives, having got a firm footing
in the trade, being acute fellows, soon became as good
workmen as any we have, and supply the foreign

manufactories with a constant recruit of artisans ; our island lying much more under pasture than any in Europe. The foreigners (notwithstanding all the restrictions the English Parliament has bound us up with) are furnished with the greatest quantity of our choicest wool. I need not tell you, sir, that a custom-house oath is held as little sacred here as in England, or that it is common for masters of vessels to swear themselves bound for one of the English wool-ports, and unload in France or Spain. By this means the trade in those ports is, in a great measure, destroyed, and we were obliged to try our hands at finer works, having only our own consumption to depend upon ; and I can assure you we have, in several kinds of narrow goods, even exceeded the English, and I believe we shall in a few years more, be able to equal them in broadcloths ; but this you may depend upon, that scarce the tenth part of English goods are now imported, of what used to be before the famous act.

The only manufactured wares we are allowed to export, are linen cloth and linen yarn, which are marketable only in England ; the rest of our commodities are wool, restrained to England, and raw hides, skins, tallow, beef, and butter. Now these are things for which the northern nations have no occasion ; we are therefore obliged, instead of carrying woollen goods to their markets, and bringing home money, to purchase their commodities.

In France, Spain, and Portugal, our wares are more valuable, though it must be owned, our fraudulent trade in wool is the best branch of our commerce ; from hence we get wines, brandy, and fruit, very cheap, and in great perfection ; so that though England has constrained us to be poor, they have given us leave to be merry. From these countries we bring home moydores, pistoles, and louisdores, without which we should scarce have a penny to turn upon.

To England we are allowed to send nothing but linen cloth, yarn, raw hides, skins, tallow, and wool. From thence we have coals, for which we always pay ready money, India goods, English woollen and silks, tobacco, hardware, earthenware, salt, and several other commodities. Our exportations to England are very much overbalanced by our importations ; so that the course of exchange is generally too high, and people choose rather to make their remittances to England in specie, than by a bill, and our nation is perpetually drained of its little running cash.

Another cause of the decay of trade, scarcity of money,

and swelling of exchange, is the unnatural affectation of our gentry to reside in and about London. Their rents are remitted to them, and spent there. The countryman wants employment from them ; the country shopkeeper wants their custom. For this reason he can't pay his Dublin correspondent readily, nor take off a great quantity of his wares. Therefore the Dublin merchant can't employ the artisan, nor keep up his credit in foreign markets.

I have discoursed some of these gentlemen, persons esteemed for good sense, and demanded a reason for this, their so unaccountable proceeding—expensive to them for the present, ruinous to their country, and destructive to the future value of their estates—and find all their answers summed up under three heads, curiosity, pleasure, and loyalty to King George. The two first excuses deserve no answer ; let us try the validity of the third. Would not loyalty be much better expressed by gentlemen staying in their respective counties, influencing their dependents by their examples, saving their own wealth, and letting their neighbours profit by their necessary expenses, thereby keeping them from misery and its unavoidable consequence, discontent ? Or is it better to flock to London, be lost in a crowd, kiss the King's hand, and take a view of the royal family ? The seeing of the royal house may animate their zeal for it ; but other advantages I know not. What employment have any of our gentlemen got by their attendance at Court, to make up to them their expenses ? Why, about forty of them have been created peers, and a little less than a hundred of them baronets and knights. For these excellent advantages, thousands of our gentry have squeezed their tenants, impoverished the trader, and impaired their own fortunes! Another great calamity is the exorbitant raising of the rents of lands. Upon the determination of all leases made before the year 1690, a gentleman thinks he has but indifferently improved his estate if he has only doubled his rent-roll. Farms are screwed up to a rack-rent—leases granted but for a small term of years—tenants tied down to hard conditions, and discouraged from cultivating the lands they occupy to the best advantage, by the certainty they have of their rent being raised on the expiration of their lease, proportionably to the improvements they shall make. Thus is honest industry restrained ; the farmer is a slave to his landlord ; 'tis well if he can cover his family with a coarse, home-spun frieze. The artisan has little dealings with him ; yet he is obliged to take his provisions from him at an extravagant price, otherwise the farmer cannot pay his rent.

The proprietors of lands keep great part of them in their own hands for sheep-pasture ; and there are thousands of poor wretches who think themselves blessed, if they can obtain a hut worse than the squire's dog-kennel, and an acre of ground for a potato plantation, on condition of being as very slaves as any in America. What can be more deplorable than to behold wretches starving in the midst of plenty ?

We are apt to charge the Irish with laziness, because we seldom find them employed ; but then we don't consider they have nothing to do.

Sir William Temple, in his excellent remarks on the United Provinces, inquires, why Holland, which has the fewest and worst ports and commodities of any nation in Europe, should abound in trade, and Ireland, which has the most and best of both, should have none ? This great man attributes this surprising accident to the natural aversion man has for labour ; who will not be persuaded to toil and fatigue himself for the superfluities of life throughout the week, when he may provide himself with all necessary subsistence by the labour of a day or two. But, with due submission to Sir William's profound judgment, the want of trade with us is rather owing to the cruel restraints we lie under, than to any disqualifications whatsoever in our inhabitants. I have not, sir, for these thirty years past, since I was concerned in trade (the greatest part of which time distresses have been flowing in upon us), ever observed them to swell so suddenly to such a height as they have done within these few months.   Our present calamities are not to be represented ; you can have no notion of them without beholding them.   Numbers of miserable objects crowd our doors, begging us to take their wares at any price, to prevent their families from immediate starving.   We cannot part with our money to them, both because we know not when we shall have vent for our goods, and as there are no debts paid, we are afraid of reducing ourselves to their lamentable circumstances.   The dismal time of trade we had during Marr's Troubles in Scotland, are looked upon as happy days when compared with the present.   I need not tell you, sir, that this griping want, this dismal poverty, this additional woe, must be put to the accursed stocks, which have desolated our country more effectually than England.   Stock-jobbing was a kind of traffic we were utterly unacquainted with. We went late to the South Sea market, and bore a great share in the losses of it, without having tasted any of its profits.

If many in England have been ruined by stocks, some have been advanced.   The English have a free and open

Q

trade to repair their losses ; but, above all, a wise, vigilant, and uncorrupted Parliament and ministry, strenuously endeavouring to restore public trade to its former happy state. Whilst we, having lost the greatest part of our cash, without any probability of its returning, must despair of retrieving our losses by trade, and have before our eyes the dismal prospect of universal poverty and desolation.

I believe, sir, you are by this time heartily tired with this indigested letter, and are firmly persuaded of the truth of what I said in the beginning of it, that you had much better have imposed this task on some of our citizens of greater abilities. But perhaps, sir, such a letter as this may be, for the singularity of it, entertaining to you, who correspond with the politest and most learned men in Europe. But I am satisfied you will excuse its want of exactness and perspicuity when you consider my education, my being unaccustomed to writings of this nature, and, above all, those calamitous objects which constantly surround us, sufficient to disturb the clearest imagination, and the soundest judgment.

Whatever cause I have given you, by this letter, to think worse of my sense and judgment, I fancy I have given you a manifest proof that I am, sir,

Your most obedient, humble servant,

J. S

"A PROPOSAL FOR THE UNIVERSAL USE OF IRISH MANUFACTURES." 1720.

THE social condition of Ireland at the above period has been already briefly described. When the landlord class were degraded and the tenantry debased by the iniquitous laws of Charles II. and William III., which suppressed the trade of the country, the oppressed people found in Swift a mouthpiece for their wrongs. The above proposal was the voice of the nation rendered articulate by his utterance. It proposes in effect a reprisal on England for her restrictions, by a refusal to use anything that comes thence. A confederation is to be formed, pledged to use nothing that is not of Irish manufacture. Everything, he trusts, will be burned that comes from England, except the people and the coals. Swift's proposal was faulty in political economy. Of this the age knew little, and Swift cared less. The printer of this pamphlet was prosecuted. The Chief Justice (Whitshed) sent back the jury nine times, and kept them eleven hours before they would consent to bring in a "special verdict." The unpopularity of the prosecution became so great that it was at last dropped.

A Proposal for the Universal Use of Irish Manufacture,

In clothes and furniture of houses, &c.

Utterly rejecting and renouncing everything wearable that comes from England. 1720.

IT is the peculiar felicity and prudence of the people in this kingdom, that whatever commodities and productions lie under the greatest discouragements from England, those are what they are sure to be most industrious in cultivating and spreading.

Agriculture, which has been the principal care of all wise nations, and for the encouragement whereof there are so many statute laws in England, we countenance so well, that the landlords are everywhere, by penal clauses, absolutely prohibiting their tenants from ploughing ;[1] not satisfied to confine them within certain

---

[1] It was the practice among the farmers to wear out their ground with ploughing, neither manuring nor letting it lie fallow ; and when their leases were nearly out, they even ploughed their meadows, so that the landlords, unable to check them by other means, were obliged to resort to this pernicious measure.

limitations, as is the practice of the English : one effect
of which is already seen in the prodigious dearness of
corn, and the importation of it from London, as the
cheaper market.   And because people are the riches of
a country, and that our neighbours have done, and are
doing, all that in them lies to make our wool a drug to
us, and a monopoly to them ; therefore, the politic
gentlemen of Ireland have depopulated vast tracts of the
best land for the feeding of sheep.

I could fill a volume as large as the history of the
Wise Men of Gotham, with a catalogue only of some
wonderful laws and customs we have observed within
thirty years past.   It is true, indeed, our beneficial
traffic of wool with France has been our only support
for several years, furnishing us with all the little money
we have to pay our rents, and go to market.   But our
merchants assure me, this trade has received a great
damp by the present fluctuating condition of the coin
in France ; and that most of their wine is paid for in
specie, without carrying thither any commodity from
hence.

However, since we are so universally bent upon en-
larging our flocks, it may be worth inquiring what we
shall do with our wool, in case Barnstaple should be
overstocked, and our French commerce should fail.

I could wish the Parliament had thought fit to have suspended their regulation of church matters, and enlargements of the prerogative, until a more convenient time, because they did not appear very pressing, at least to the persons principally concerned ; and, instead of these great refinements in politics and divinity, had amused themselves and their committees a little with the state of the nation. For example : What if the House of Commons had thought fit to make a resolution, *nemine contradicente*, against wearing any cloth or stuff in their families, which were not of the growth and manufacture of this kingdom ? What if they had extended it so far as utterly to exclude all silks, velvets, calicoes, and the whole lexicon of female fopperies ; and declared, that whoever acted otherwise should be deemed and reputed an enemy to the nation ? What if they had sent up such a resolution to be agreed to by the House of Lords, and by their own practice and encouragement, spread the execution of it in their several countries ? What if we should agree to make burying in woollen a fashion, as our neighbours have made it a law? What if the ladies would be content with Irish stuffs for the furniture of their houses, for gowns and petticoats for themselves and their daughters ? Upon the whole, and to crown all the rest, let a firm resolution be taken, by male and female, never to appear with one single shred that comes from England, and let all the people say AMEN.

I hope and believe, that nothing could please his Majesty better than to hear that his loyal subjects of both sexes in this kingdom celebrated his birthday (now approaching) universally clad in their own manufacture. Is there virtue enough left in this deluded people to save them from the brink of ruin? If men's opinions may be taken, the ladies will look as handsome in stuffs as in brocades; and since all will be equal, there may be room enough to employ their wit and fancy, in choosing and matching patterns and colours.

I heard the late Archbishop of Tuam mention a pleasant observation of somebody's, that Ireland would never be happy, till a law were made for burning everything that came from England, except their people and their coals.

I must confess, that as to the former, I should not be sorry if they would stay at home; and for the latter, I hope in a little time we shall have no occasion for them.

> Non tanti mitra est, non tanti judicis ostrum—

but I should rejoice to see a stay-lace from England

be thought scandalous, and become a topic for censure at visits and tea-tables.

If the unthinking shopkeepers in this town had not been utterly destitute of common sense, they would have made some proposal to the Parliament, with a petition to the purpose I have mentioned ; promising to improve the cloths and stuffs of the nation into all possible degrees of fineness and colours, and engaging not to play the knave, according to their custom, by exacting and imposing upon the nobility and gentry, either as to the prices or the goodness.

For I remember, in London, upon a general mourning, the rascally mercers and woollen-drapers would in twenty-four hours raise their cloths and silks to above a double price, and if the mourning continued long, then come whining with petitions to the court, that they were ready to starve, and their fineries lay upon their hands.

I could wish our shopkeepers would immediately think on this proposal, addressing it to all persons of quality and others ; but, first, be sure to get somebody who can write sense, to put it into form.

I think it needless to exhort the clergy to follow this good example ; because, in a little time, those among them who are so unfortunate as to have had their birth and education in this country, will think themselves

abundantly happy when they can afford Irish crape, and
an Athlone hat ; and as to the others, I shall not presume to direct them.   I have, indeed, seen the present
Archbishop of Dublin clad from head to foot in our own
manufacture ; and yet, under the rose be it spoken, his
Grace deserves as good a gown as if he had not been
born among us.

I have not courage enough to offer one syllable on
this subject to their honours of the army ; neither have
I sufficiently considered the great importance of scarlet
and gold lace.

The fable in Ovid of Arachne and Pallas is to this
purpose.—The goddess had heard of one Arachne, a
young virgin, very famous for spinning and weaving.
They both met upon a trial of skill ; and Pallas, finding
herself almost equalled in her own art, stung with rage
and envy, knocked her rival down, and turned her
into a spider ; enjoining her to spin and weave for
ever out of her own bowels, and in a very narrow
compass.

I confess, that, from a boy, I always pitied poor
Arachne, and could never heartily love the goddess, on
account of so cruel and unjust a sentence ; which, however, is fully executed upon us by England, with farther
additions of rigour and severity ; for the greatest part

of our bowels and vitals is extracted, without allowing us the liberty of spinning and weaving them.

The Scripture tells us, that "oppression makes a wise man mad;" therefore, consequently speaking, the reason why some men are not mad is because they are not wise. However it were to be wished, that oppression would in time teach a little wisdom to fools.

I was much delighted with a person, who has a great estate in this kingdom, upon his complaints to me, how grievously poor England suffers by impositions from Ireland :—That we convey our wool to France, in spite of all the harpies at the custom-house ; that Mr. Shuttleworth and others, on the Cheshire coast, are such fools to sell us their bark at a good price for tanning our own hides into leather ; with other enormities of the like weight and kind. To which I will venture to add more :—That the mayoralty of this city is always executed by an inhabitant, and often by a native, which might as well be done by a deputy with a moderate salary, whereby poor England loses at least one thousand pounds a-year upon the balance ; that the governing of this kingdom costs the Lord-Lieutenant three thousand six hundred pounds a year—so much net loss to poor England ; that the people of Ireland presume to dig for coals on their own grounds; and the farmers in the county of Wicklow send their turf to the very market of Dublin, to the great discouragement of the coal trade of Mostyn and Whitehaven ; that the revenues of the post-office here, so righteously belonging to the English treasury, as arising chiefly from our commerce with each other, should be remitted to London clogged with that grievous burden of exchange ; and the pensions paid out of the Irish revenues to English favourites, should lie under the same disadvantage, to the great loss of the grantees. When a divine is sent over to a bishopric here, with the hopes of five and-twenty hundred pounds a year, and, upon his arrival, he finds, alas ! a dreadful discount of ten or twelve per cent.; a judge, or a commissioner of the revenue, has the same cause of complaint. . . . These are a few among the many hardships we put upon that poor kingdom of England, for which, I am confident, every honest man wishes a remedy. And I hear there is a project on foot for transporting our best wheaten straw, by sea and land carriage, to Dunstable, and obliging us, by a law, to take off yearly so many ton of straw hats, for the use of our women ; which will be a great encouragement to the manufacture of that industrious town.

I should be glad to learn among the divines, whether a law to bind men without their own consent be obligatory *in foro conscientiæ*; because I find Scripture, Sanderson, and Suarez, are wholly silent on the matter. The oracle of reason, the great law of nature, and general opinion of civilians, wherever they treat of limited governments, are indeed decisive enough.

It is wonderful to observe the bias among our people in favour of things, persons, and wares of all kinds, that come from England. The printer tells his hawkers, that he has got an excellent new song just brought from London. I have somewhat of a tendency that way myself; and, upon hearing a cox-comb from thence displaying himself, with great volu-bility, upon the park, the playhouse, the opera, the gaming ordinaries, it was apt to beget in me a kind of veneration for his parts and accomplishments. It is not many years since I remember a person, who, by his style and literature, seems to have been the corrector of a hedge-press in some blind alley about Little Britain, proceed gradually to be an author, at least a translator of a lower rate, although somewhat of a larger bulk, than any that now flourishes in Grub Street; and, upon the strength of this foundation, come over here, erect himself up into an orator and politician, and lead a kingdom after him. This, I am told, was the very motive that prevailed on the author

of a play, called "Love in a Hollow Tree," to do us
the honour of a visit; presuming, with very good
reason, that he was a writer of a superior class. I
know another, who, for thirty years past, has been the
common standard of stupidity in England, where he
was never heard a minute in any assembly, or by any
party, with common Christian treatment; yet, upon his
arrival here, could put on a face of importance and
authority, talk more than six, without either graceful-
ness, propriety, or meaning, and, at the same time, be
admired and followed as the pattern of eloquence and
wisdom.

.·   ·   ·   ·   ·   ·

I would now expostulate a little with our country
landlords; who, by unmeasurable screwing and racking
their tenants all over the kingdom, have already reduced
the miserable people to a worse condition than the pea-
sants in France, or the vassals in Germany and Poland;
so that the whole species of what we call substantial
farmers, will, in a very few years, be utterly at an end.
It was pleasant to observe these gentlemen labouring,
with all their might, for preventing the bishops from
letting their revenues at a moderate half value (whereby
the whole order would, in an age, have been reduced
to manifest beggary), at the very instant when

they were everywhere canting[2] their own land upon short leases, and sacrificing their oldest tenants for a penny an acre advance. . . . I have heard great divines affirm, that nothing is so likely to call down a universal judgment from Heaven upon a nation as universal oppression ; and whether this be not already verified in part, their worships the landlords, are now at full leisure to consider. Whoever travels this country, and observes the face of nature, or the faces, and habits, and dwellings of the natives, will hardly think himself in a land where law, religion, or common humanity is professed. I cannot forbear saying one word upon a thing they call a bank, which, I fear, is projecting in this town.[3] I never saw the proposals, nor understood any one particular of their scheme. What I wish for at present, is only a sufficient provision of hemp, and caps and bells, to distribute according to the several degrees of honesty and prudence in some persons. I hear only of a monstrous sum already named ; and if others do not soon hear of it too, and hear with a vengeance, then I am a gentleman of less sagacity than myself, and very few beside myself, take me to be. And the jest will be still

---

[2] Putting up at auction.

[3] A project for establishing an Irish Bank, which was soon after placed before Parliament, but rejected.

the better if it be true, as judicious persons have assured me, that one half of this money will be real, and the other half altogether imaginary. The matter will be likewise much mended, if the merchants continue to carry off our gold, and our goldsmiths to melt down our heavy silver.

THIS came out when the people were starving in hundreds through famine, and the dead were left unburied before their own doors. English civilization was shamed by the sight. His sarcasm was never applied with more deadly seriousness of purpose. There is no strain in the language with which the state of matters is described : the very simplicity and matter-of-fact tone that are assumed, make the description all the more telling. With the calm deliberation of a statistician calculating the food supply of the country, Swift brings forward his suggestion. No work of Swift has been more grievously misunderstood. Some have esteemed it a heartless piece of ridicule, a callous laugh raised out of abject misery. The interpretation is as wrong as the Frenchman who took it as a grave and practical suggestion, and who fancied that Swift in sober earnest proposed that infants in Ireland should be used for food. In truth the ridicule is but a thin disguise. From beginning to end, it is laden with grave and torturing bitterness. Each touch, if calm and ghastly human, is added with the gravity of a surgeon who probes a wound to the quick. There is nothing like it in all literature.

A MODEST PROPOSAL

For preventing the children of poor people in Ireland from being a burden to their parents or country, and for making them beneficial to the public. 1729.

IT is a melancholy object to those who walk through this great town, or travel in the country, when they see the streets, the roads, and cabin doors, crowded with beggars of the female sex, followed by three, four, or six children, all in rags, and importuning every passenger for an alms. These mothers, instead of being able to work for an honest livelihood, are forced to employ all their time in strolling to beg sustenance for their helpless infants ; who, as they grow up, either turn thieves for the want of work, or leave their dear native country to fight for the Pretender in Spain, or sell themselves to the Barbadoes.

I think it is agreed by all parties, that this prodigious number of children in the arms, or on the backs, or at the heels of their mothers, and frequently of their fathers,

R

is, in the present deplorable state of the kingdom, a very great additional grievance ; and, therefore, whoever could find out a fair, cheap, and easy method of making these children sound, useful members of the commonwealth, would deserve so well of the public, as to have his statue set up for a preserver of the nation.

But my intention is very far from being confined to provide only for the children of professed beggars ; it is of a much greater extent, and shall take in the whole number of infants at a certain age, who are born of parents in effect as little able to support them, as those who demand charity in our streets.

As to my own part, having turned my thoughts for many years upon this important subject, and maturely weighed the several schemes of our projectors, I have always found them grossly mistaken in their computation. It is true, a child, just dropped from its dam, may be supported by her milk for a solar year, with little other nourishment ; at most, not above the value of two shillings, which the mother may certainly get, or the value in scraps, by her lawful occupation of begging ; and it is exactly at one year old that I propose to provide for them in such a manner, as, instead of being a charge upon their parents, or the parish, or wanting food and raiment for the rest of their lives, they shall, on the contrary, contribute to the feeding, and partly to the clothing, of many thousands. . . .

The number of souls in this kingdom being usually reckoned one million and a half, of these I calculate there may be about two hundred thousand couple whose wives are breeders ; from which number I subtract thirty thousand couple, who are able to maintain their own children, (although I apprehend there cannot be so many, under the present distresses of the kingdom) ; but this being granted, there will remain a hundred and seventy thousand breeders. I again subtract fifty thousand for those women who miscarry, or whose children die by accident or disease within the year. There only remains a hundred and twenty thousand children of poor parents annually born. The question therefore is : How this number shall be reared and provided for ?—which, as I have already said, under the present situation of affairs, is utterly impossible by all the methods hitherto proposed. For we can neither employ them in handicraft or agriculture ; we neither build houses (I mean in the country) nor cultivate land ; they can very seldom pick up a livelihood by stealing, till they arrive at six years old, except where they are of towardly parts; although I confess they learn the rudiments much earlier ; during which time they can, however, be properly looked upon only as probationers ; as I have been informed by a principal gentleman in the county of Cavan, who protested to me, that he never knew above one or two instances under the age of six, even in a part of the kingdom so renowned for the quickest proficiency in that art.

I am assured by our merchants, that a boy or girl before twelve years old is no saleable commodity ; and even when they come to this age, they will not yield above three pounds, or three pounds and half-a-crown at most, on the exchange ; which cannot turn to account either to the parents or kingdom, the charge of nutriment and rags having been at least four times that value. I shall now, therefore, humbly propose my own thoughts, which I hope will not be liable to the least objection.

I have been assured by a very knowing American of my acquaintance in London, that a young healthy child, well nursed, is, at a year old, a most delicious, nourishing, and wholesome food, whether stewed, roasted, baked or boiled ; and I make no doubt that it will equally serve in a fricassee or a ragout.

I do therefore humbly offer it to public consideration, that of the hundred and twenty thousand children already computed, twenty thousand may be reserved for breed. That the remaining hundred thousand may, at a year old, be offered in sale to the persons of quality and fortune through the kingdom; always advising the mother to let them suck plentifully in the last month, so as to render them plump and fat for a good table. A child will make two dishes at an entertainment for friends; and when the family dines alone, the fore or hind quarter will make a reasonable dish, and, seasoned with a little pepper or salt, will be very good boiled on the fourth day, especially in winter.

I have reckoned, upon a medium, that a child just born will weigh twelve pounds, and in a solar year, if tolerably nursed, will increase to twenty-eight pounds. I grant this food will be somewhat dear, and therefore very proper for landlords, who, as they have already devoured most of the parents, seem to have the best title to the children. . . .

I have already computed the charge of nursing a beggar's child (in which list I reckon all cottagers, labourers, and four-fifths of the farmers) to be about two shillings per annum, rags included; and I believe no gentleman would require to give ten shillings for the carcass of a good fat child, which, as I have said, will make four dishes of excellent nutritive meat, when he has only some particular friend, or his own family to dine with him. Thus the squire will learn to be a good landlord, and grow popular among his tenants ; and the mother will have eight shillings net profit.

Those who are more thrifty (as I must confess that times require) may flay the carcass ; the skin of which, artificially dressed, will make admirable gloves for ladies, and summer boots for fine gentlemen. As to our city of Dublin, shambles may be appointed for this purpose in the most convenient parts of it, and butchers we may be assured will not be wanting ; although I rather recommend buying the children alive, then dressing them hot from the knife, as we do roasting pigs.

A very worthy person, a true lover of his country, and whose virtue I highly esteem, was lately pleased, in discoursing on this matter, to offer a refinement upon my scheme. He said, that many gentlemen of this kingdom, having of late destroyed their deer, he conceived that the want of venison might be well supplied by the bodies of young lads and maidens, not exceeding fourteen years of age, nor under twelve ; so great a number of both sexes in every country being now ready to starve for want of work and service ; and these to be disposed of by their parents, if alive, or otherwise by their nearest relations. But, with due deference to so excellent a friend, and so deserving a patriot, I cannot be altogether in his sentiments ; for as to the males, my American acquaintance assured me, from frequent experience, that their flesh was generally tough and lean like that of our schoolboys, by continual exercise, and their taste disagreeable ; and to fatten them would not answer the charge ; and besides, it is not improbable that some scrupulous people might be apt to censure such a practice (although indeed very unjustly), as a little bordering upon cruelty ; which, I confess, has always been with me the strongest objection against any project, how well soever intended.

But in order to justify my friend, he confessed that this expedient was put into his head by the famous Psalmanazar, a native of the island Formosa, who came from thence to London above twenty years ago ; and in conversation told my friend, that in his country, when any young person happened to be put to death the executioner sold the carcass to persons of quality as a prime dainty ; and that in his time the body of a plump girl of fifteen, who was crucified for an attempt to poison the emperor, was sold to his imperial Majesty's prime minister of state, and other great mandarins of the court, in joints from the gibbet, at four hundred crowns.

Neither indeed can I deny, that if the same use were

made of several plump young girls in this town, who without one single groat to their fortunes, cannot stir abroad without a chair, and appear at playhouse and assemblies in foreign fineries which they will never pay for, the kingdom would not be the worse.

Some persons of a desponding spirit are in great concern about that vast number of poor people, who are aged, diseased, or maimed ; and I have been desired to employ my thoughts, what course may be taken to ease the nation of so grievous an encumbrance. But I am not in the least pain upon that matter, because it is very well known, that they are every day dying by cold and famine, as fast as can be reasonably expected. And as to the young labourers, they are now in almost as hopeful a condition : they cannot get work, and consequently pine away for want of nourishment, to a degree, that if at any time they are accidentally hired to common labour, they have not strength to perform it; and thus the country and themselves are happily delivered from the evils to come.

I have too long digressed, and therefore shall return to my subject. I think the advantages by the proposal which I have made, are obvious and many, as well as of the highest importance.

For first, it would greatly lessen the number of

Papists, with whom we are yearly overrun, being the principal breeders of the nation, as well as our most dangerous enemies, and who stay at home on purpose to deliver the kingdom to the Pretender, hoping to take their advantage by the absence of so many good Protestants, who have chosen rather to leave their country than stay at home and pay tithes against their conscience to an Episcopal curate.

Secondly, The poorer tenants will have something valuable of their own, which by law may be made liable to distress, and help to pay their landlord's rent; their corn and cattle being already seized, and money a thing unknown.

Thirdly, Whereas the maintenance of a hundred thousand children, from two years old and upward, cannot be computed at less than ten shillings a-piece per annum, the nation's stock will be thereby increased fifty thousand pounds per annum, beside the profit of a new dish introduced to the tables of all gentlemen of fortune in the kingdom, who have any refinement in taste. And the money will circulate among ourselves, the goods being entirely of our own growth and manufacture.

Fourthly, The constant breeders, besides the gain of eight shillings sterling per annum by the sale of their children, will be rid of the charge of maintaining them after the first year.

Fifthly, This food would likewise bring great custom to taverns ; where the vintners will certainly be so prudent as to procure the best receipts for dressing it to perfection, and, consequently, have their houses frequented by all the fine gentlemen, who justly value themselves upon their knowledge in good eating ; and a skilful cook, who understands how to oblige his guests, will contrive to make it as expensive as they please.

Sixthly, This would be a great inducement to marriage, which all wise nations have either encouraged by rewards, or enforced by laws and penalties. It would increase the care and tenderness of mothers towards their children, when they were sure of a settlement for life to the poor babes, provided in some sort by the public, to their annual profit or expense. We should see an honest emulation among the married women, which of them could bring the fattest child to the market. . . .

I can think of no one objection, that will possibly be raised against this proposal, unless it should be urged that the number of people will be thereby much lessened in the kingdom. This I freely own, and it was indeed one principal design in offering it to the world. I desire the reader will observe that I calculate my remedy for

this one individual kingdom of Ireland, and for no other
that ever was, is, or, I think, ever can be, upon earth.
Therefore let no man talk to me of other expedients :
of taxing our absentees at five shillings a pound ; of
using neither clothes, nor household furniture, except
what is our own growth and manufacture ; of utterly
rejecting the materials and instruments that promote
foreign luxury ; of curing the expensiveness of pride,
vanity, idleness, and gaming in our women : of intro-
ducing a vein of parsimony, prudence, and temperance ;
of learning to love our country, in the want of which we
differ even from Laplanders, and the inhabitants of
Topinamboo ; of quitting our animosities and factions,
nor acting any longer like the Jews, who were murder-
ing one another at the very moment their city was
taken ; of being a little cautious not to sell our country
and conscience for nothing ; of teaching landlords to
have at least one degree of mercy toward their tenants :
lastly, of putting a spirit of honesty, industry, and skill
into our shopkeepers ; who, if a resolution could now be
taken to buy only our negative goods, would immediately
unite to cheat and exact upon us in the price, the
measure, and the goodness, nor could never yet be
brought to make one fair proposal of just dealing, though
often and earnestly invited to it.

Therefore I repeat, let no man talk to me of these and the like expedients, till he has at least some glimpse of hope that there will be ever some hearty and sincere attempt to put them in practice.

But as to myself, having been wearied out for many years with offering vain, idle, visionary thoughts, and at length utterly despairing of success, I fortunately fell upon this proposal; which as it is wholly new, so it has something solid and real, of no expense and little trouble, full in our own power, and whereby we can incur no danger in disobliging England. For this kind of commodity will not bear exportation, the flesh being of too tender a consistence to admit a long continuance in salt, although perhaps I could name a country which would be glad to eat up our whole nation without.

After all, I am not so violently bent upon my own opinion as to reject any offer proposed by wise men, which shall be found equally innocent, cheap, easy, and effectual. But before something of that kind shall be advanced in contradiction to my scheme, and offering a better, I desire the author or authors will be pleased maturely to consider two points. First, as things now stand, how they will be able to find food and raiment for a hundred thousand useless mouths and backs. And, secondly, there being a round million of creatures of

human figure throughout this kingdom, whose whole subsistence put into a common stock would leave them in
debt two millions of pounds sterling, adding those who
are beggars by profession, to the bulk of farmers, cottagers, and labourers, with the wives and children who
are beggars in effect. I desire those politicians who
dislike my overture, and may perhaps be so bold as to
attempt an answer, that they will first ask the parents of
these mortals, whether they would not at this day think
it a great happiness to have been sold for food at a year
old, in the manner I prescribe, and thereby have avoided
a perpetual scene of misfortunes, as they have since gone
through, by the oppression of landlords, the impossibility
of paying rent without money or trade, the want of
common sustenance, with neither house nor clothes to
cover them from the inclemencies of the weather, and the
most inevitable prospect of entailing the like, or greater
miseries, upon their breed for ever.

I profess, in the sincerity of my heart, that I have not the
least personal interest in endeavouring to promote this
necessary work, having no other motive than the public
good of my country, by advancing our trade, providing
for infants, relieving the poor, and giving some pleasure
to the rich. I have no children by which I can propose
to get a single penny ; the youngest being nine years old
and my wife past child-bearing.

A CHARACTER, PANEGYRIC, AND DESCRIPTION OF THE LEGION CLUB, 1736.

SWIFT levelled his heaviest invective against the corrupt practices of the so-called Irish Parliament, which did not contain a single representative of the people who comprised the bulk of the nation. The colonial representation were of the most degraded order, most of the characters described in the poem were hit off with caustic precision. The portraits were so true to life that many recognized themselves. The piece is generally accepted as a good skit on the House.

A CHARACTER, PANEGYRIC, AND DESCRIPTION OF THE LEGION CLUB, 1736.

As I stroll the city, oft I
See a building large and lofty,
Not a bow-shot from the college ;
Half the globe from sense and knowledge :

By the prudent architect,
Placed against the church direct,
Making good my granddam's jest,
"Near the church,"—you know the rest.

Tell us what the pile contains?
Many a head that holds no brains,
These demoniacs let me dub
With the name of Legion Club.
Such assemblies, you might swear,
Meet when butchers bait a bear :
Such a noise, and such haranguing,
When a brother thief is hanging ;
Such a rout and such a rabble
Run to hear Jackpudding gabble.

Could I from the building's top
Hear the rattling thunder drop,
While the devil upon the roof
(If the devil be thunder-proof)
Should with poker fiery red
Crack the stones, and melt the lead ;
Drive them down on every skull,
When the den of thieves is full ;
Quite destroy that harpies' nest ;
How might then our isle be blest !

For divines allow, that God
Sometimes makes the devil his rod ;
And the gospel will inform us,
He can punish sins enormous.

Yet should Swift endow the schools,
For his lunatics and fools,
With a rood or two of land,
I allow the pile may stand.
You perhaps will ask me, Why so ?
But it is with this proviso ;
Since the house is like to last,
Let the royal grant be pass'd,
That the club have right to dwell
Each within his proper cell,
With a passage left to creep in,
And a hole above for peeping.

Let them, when they once get in,
Sell the nation for a pin ;
While they sit a-picking straws,
Let them rave at making laws ;
Let them form a grand committee,
How to plague and starve the city ;
Let them stare, and storm, and frown,
When they see a clergy gown ;

Let them, with their gosling quills,
Scribble senseless heads of bills.

. . . . . .

Come, assist me, Muse obedient !
Let us try some new expedient ;
Shift the scene for half an hour,
Time and place are in thy power.
Thither, gentle Muse, conduct me ;
I shall ask, and you instruct me.
See, the Muse unbars the gate ;
Hark, the monkeys, how they prate !
All ye gods who rule the soul ;
Styx, through Hell whose waters roll !
Let me be allowed to tell
What I heard in yonder Hell.

Near the door an entrance gapes,
Crowded round with antic shapes,
Poverty, and Grief, and Care,
Causeless Joy, and true Despair ;
Discord periwigg'd with snakes,
See the dreadful strides she takes !
By this odious crew beset,
I began to rage and fret,

S

And resolved to break their pates,
Ere we entered at the gates ;
Had not Clio in the nick
Whispered me, " Lay down your stick."
What! said I, is this the madhouse ?
These, she answer'd, are but shadows,
Phantoms bodiless and vain,
Empty visions of the brain.

In the porch Briareus stands,
Shows a bribe in all his hands ;
Briareus the secretary,
But we mortals call him Carey.[1]
When the rogues their country fleece,
They may hope for pence a-piece,

Clio, who had been so wise
To put on a fool's disguise,
To bespeak some approbation,
And be thought a near relation,
When she saw three hundred brutes
All involved in wild disputes,
Roaring till their lungs were spent,
PRIVILEGE OF PARLIAMENT,

[1] The Right Honourable Walter Carey. He was Secretary to
the Duke of Dorset when Lord-Lieutenant of Ireland.

Now a new misfortune feels,
Dreading to be laid by th' heels.
Never durst a Muse before
Enter that infernal door:
Clio, stifled with the smell,
Into spleen and vapours fell,
By the Stygian steams that flew
From the dire infectious crew.
Not the stench of Lake Avernus
Could have more offended her nose
Had she flown but o'er the top,
She had felt her pinions drop.
And by exhalations dire,
Though a goddess, must expire.
In a fright she crept away,
Bravely I resolved to stay.
When I saw the keeper frown,
Tipping him with half-a-crown,
Now, said I, we are alone,
Name your heroes one by one,

Who is that hell-featured brawler?
Is it Satan ?ʼ No, 'tis Waller.
In what figure can a bard dress
Jack the grandson of Sir Hardress ?

Honest keeper, drive him further,
In his looks are Hell and murther ;
See the scowling visage drop,
Just as when he murder'd Throp.
Keeper, show me where to fix
On the puppy pair of Dicks :
By their lantern jaws and leathern,
You might swear they both are brethren :
Dick Fitzbaker, Dick the player,
Old acquaintance are you there ?
Tie them, keeper, in a tether,
Let them starve and sink together ;
Both are apt to be unruly,
Lash them daily, lash them duly ;
Though 'tis hopeless to reclaim them,
Scorpion rods, perhaps, may tame them.
Keeper, yon old dotard smoke,
Sweetly snoring in his cloak :
Who is he ?   'Tis humdrum Wynne,
Half encompassed by his kin :
There observe the tribe of Bingham,
For he never fails to bring 'em ;
While he sleeps the whole debate,
They submissive round him wait ;
Yet would gladly see the hunks,

In his grave, and search his trunks,

See, they gently twitch his coat,

Just to yawn and give his vote,

Always firm in his vocation,

For the court against the nation.

Those are Allens Jack and Bob,

First in every wicked job,

Son and brother to a queer

Brain-sick brute, they call a peer.

We must give them better quarter

For their ancestor trod mortar,

And at Hoath, to boast his fame,

On a chimney cut his name.

There sit Clements, Dilks, and Harrison ;

How they swagger from their garrison !

Such a triplet could you tell

Where to find on this side Hell ?

Harrison, and Dilks, and Clements,

Keeper, see they have their payments,

Every mischief's in their hearts ;

If they fail 'tis want of parts.

Bless us ! Morgan, art thou there, man ?

Bless mine eyes ! art thou the chairman ?

Chairman to yon damn'd committee !
Yet I look on thee with pity.
Dreadful sight ! what, learned Morgan
Metamorphosed to a Gorgon !
For thy horrid looks, I own,
Half convert me to a stone.
Hast thou been so long at school,
Now to turn a factious tool ?
Alma Mater was thy mother,
Every young divine thy brother.
Thou ungrateful to thy teachers,
Who are all grown reverend preachers !
Morgan, would it not surprise one !
Turn thy nourishment to poison !
When you walk among your books,
They reproach you with their looks ;
Bind them fast, or from their shelves
They will come and right themselves :
Homer, Plutarch, Virgil, Flaccus,
All in arms prepare to back us ;
Soon repent, or put to slaughter
Every Greek and Roman author.
Will you, in your faction's phras e,
Send the clergy all to graze ;
And to make your project pass,

Leave them not a blade of grass?
Now I want thee, humorous Hogarth!
Thou, I hear, a pleasant rogue art.
Were but you and I acquainted,
Every monster should be painted:
You should try your graving tools
On this odious group of fools;
Draw the beasts as I describe them:
From their features while I gibe them;
Draw them like; for I assure you,
You will need no *car'catura*;
Draw them so that we may trace
All the soul in every face.

Keeper, I must now retire,
You have done what I desire:
But I feel my spirits spent
With the noise, the sight, the scent.
"Pray, be patient; you shall find
Half the best are still behind!
You have hardly seen a score;
I can show two hundred more."
Keeper, I have seen enough,
Taking then a pinch of snuff,
I concluded, looking round them,
"May their god, the devil, confound them!"

ON DOING GOOD.

A Sermon on the Occasion of Wood's Project.

(WRITTEN IN 1724.)

"As we have therefore opportunity, let us do good unto all men." (GALATIANS vi. 10.)

NATURE directs every one of us, and God permits us, to consult our own private good, before the private good of any other person whatsoever. We are, indeed, commanded to love our neighbour as ourselves, but not as well as ourselves. The love we have for ourselves, is to be the pattern of that love we ought to have toward our neighbour; but as the copy doth not equal the original, so my neighbour cannot think it hard, if I prefer myself, who am the original, before him, who is only the copy. Thus, if any matter equally concern the life, the reputation, the profit of my neighbour and my own; the law of nature, which is the law of God, obligeth me to take care of myself first, and afterward of him. And this I need not be at much pains in persuading you to; for the want of self-love, with regard to things of this world, is not among the faults of mankind. But then, on the other side, if, by a small hurt and loss to myself, I can procure a great good to my neighbour, in that case his interest is to be preferred. For example, if I can be sure of saving his life, without great danger to my own ; if I can preserve him from being undone without ruining myself; or recover his reputation without blasting mine ; all this I am obliged to do, and if I sincerely perform it, I do then obey the command of God, in loving my neighbour as myself.

But, besides this love we owe to every man in his particular capacity, under the title of our neighbour, there is yet a duty of a more large extensive nature incumbent on us ; our love to our neighbour in his public capacity, as he is a member of that great body the commonwealth, under the same government with ourselves ; and this is usually called love of the public, and is a duty to which we are more strictly obliged, than even that of loving ourselves ; because therein ourselves are also contained, as well as all our neighbours, in one great body. This love of the public, or of the commonwealth, or love of our country, was in ancient times properly known by the name of virtue, because it was the greatest of all virtues, and was supposed to contain all virtues in it ; and many great examples of this virtue are left us on record, scarcely to be believed or even conceived, in such a base, corrupted, wicked age as this we live in.   In those times it was common for men to sacrifice their lives for the good of their country, although they had neither hope nor belief of future rewards ; whereas, in our days, very few make the least scruple of sacrificing a whole nation, as well as their own souls, for a little present gain ; which often hath been known to end in their own ruin in this world ; as it certainly must in that to come.   Have we not seen men, for the sake of some petty employment, give up the very natural rights and liberties of their country, and of man- kind, in the ruin of which themselves must at last be involved ?   Are not these corruptions gotten among the meanest of our people, who, for a piece of money, will give their votes at a venture, for the disposal of their own lives and fortunes, without considering whether it be to those who are most likely to betray or defend them ?   But, if I were to produce only one instance of a hundred, wherein we fail in this duty of loving our country, it would be an endless labour, and therefore I shall not attempt it.

But here I would not be misunderstood ; by the love of our country, I do not mean loyalty to our King, for that is a duty of another nature ; and a man may be very loyal, in the common sense of the word, without one grain of public good at his heart.

Witness this very kingdom we live in. I verily believe, that since the beginning of the world, no nation upon earth ever showed (all circumstances considered) such high constant marks of loyalty, in all their actions and behaviour, as we have done ; and, at the same time, no people ever appeared more utterly void of what is called a public spirit. When I say the people, I mean the bulk or mass of the people, for I have nothing to do with those in power. Therefore I shall think my time not ill-spent, if I can persuade most or all of you who hear me, to show the love you have for your country, by endeavouring, in your several situations, to do all the public good you are able.

For I am certainly persuaded, that all our misfortunes arise from no other original cause than that general disregard among us to the public welfare. I therefore undertake to show you three things :—

First, That there are few people so weak or mean, who have it not sometimes in their power to be useful to the public.

Secondly, That it is often in the power of the meanest among mankind to do mischief to the public.

And, *lastly*, That all wilful injuries done to the public,

are very great and aggravated sins in the sight of God.

First, There are few people so weak or mean, who have it not sometimes in their power to be useful to the public.

Solomon tells us of a poor wise man, who saved a city by his counsel. It hath often happened that a private soldier, by some unexpected brave attempt, hath been instrumental in obtaining a great victory. How many obscure men have been authors of very useful inventions, whereof the world now reaps the benefit. The very example of honesty and industry in a poor tradesman, will sometimes spread through a neighbourhood, when others see how successful he is ; and thus so many useful members are gained, for which the whole body of the public is the better. Whoever is blessed with a true public spirit, God will certainly put it in his way to make use of that blessing, for the ends it was given him, by some means or other : and therefore it hath been observed, in most ages that the greatest actions for the benefit of the commonwealth, have been performed by the wisdom or courage, the contrivance or industry, of ·particular men, and not of numbers, and that the safety of a kingdom hath often been owing to those hands whence it was least expected.

But, *secondly*, It is often in the power of the meanest amnog mankind to do mischief to the public, and hence arise most of those miseries with which the states and kingdoms of the earth are infested. How many great princes have been murdered by the meanest ruffians !

The weakest hand can open a flood-gate to drown a country, which a thousand of the strongest cannot stop. Those who have thrown off all regard for public good, will often have it in their way to do public evil, and will not fail to exercise that power whenever they can.

The greatest blow given of late to this kingdom, was by the dishonesty of a few manufacturers ; by imposing bad wares at foreign markets, in almost the only traffic permitted to us, did half ruin that trade ; by which this poor unhappy kingdom still suffers in the midst of sufferings. I speak not here of persons in high stations who ought to be free from all reflection, and are supposed always to intend the welfare of the community : but we now find by experience, that the meanest instrument may, by the concurrence of accidents, have it in his power to bring a whole kingdom to the very brink of destruction, and is at this present endeavouring to finish his work ; and hath agents among ourselves who are contented to see their own country undone, to be small sharers in that iniquitous gain, which at last must end in their own ruin, as well as ours.   I confess it was chiefly the consideration of that great danger we are in, which engaged me to discourse to you on this subject, to exhort you to a love of your country, and a public spirit, when all you have is at stake ; to prefer the interest of your prince and your fellow-subjects, before that of one destructive impostor, and a few of his adherents.

Perhaps it may be thought by some, that this way of discoursing is not so proper from the pulpit.   But, surely, when an open attempt is made, and far carried on, to make a great kingdom one large poorhouse, to deprive us of all means to exercise hospitality or charity, to turn our cities and churches into ruins, to make the country a desert for wild beasts and robbers, to destroy all arts and sciences, all trades and manufactures, and the very tillage of the ground, only to enrich one obscure, ill-designing projector and his followers ; it is time for the pastor to cry out, "that the wolf is getting into his flock," to warn them to stand together, and all to consult the common safety.   And God be praised for His infinite goodness in raising such a spirit of union among us, at least in this point, in the midst of all our former divisions ; which union, if it continue, will in all probability defeat the pernicious design of this pestilent enemy to the nation !

But hence it clearly follows how necessary the love of our country, or a public spirit, is, in every particular man, since the wicked have so many opportunities of doing public mischief. Every man is upon his guard for his private advantage ; but where the public is concerned, he is apt to be negligent, considering himself as only one among two or three millions, among whom the loss is equally shared ; and thus, he thinks, he can be no great sufferer. Meanwhile the trader, the farmer, and the shopkeeper, complain of the hardness and deadness of the times, and wonder whence it comes ; while it is in a great measure owing to their own folly, for want of that love of their country, and public spirit and firm union among themselves, which are so necessary to the prosperity of every nation.

Another method, by which the meanest wicked man may have it in his power to injure the public, is false accusation ; whereof this kingdom hath afforded too many examples ; neither is it long since no man, whose opinions were thought to differ from those in fashion could safely converse beyond his nearest friends, for fear of being sworn against, as a traitor, by those who made a traffic of perjury and subornation ; by which the very peace of the nation was disturbed, and men fled from each other as they would from a lion or a bear got loose.

And it is very remarkable, that the pernicious project now in hand, to reduce us to beggary, was forwarded by one of these false accusers, who had been convicted of endeavouring, by perjury and subornation, to take away the lives of several innocent persons here among us ; and, indeed, there could not be a more proper instrument for such a work.

Another method, by which the meanest people may do injury to the public, is the spreading of lies and false rumours ; thus raising a distrust among the people of a nation, causing them to mistake their true interest, and their enemies for their friends ; and this hath been likewise too successful a practice among us, where we have known the whole kingdom misled by the grossest lies, raised upon occasion to serve some particular turn. As it hath also happened in the case I lately mentioned, where one obscure man, by representing our wants where they were least, and concealing them where they were greatest, had almost succeeded in a project of utterly ruining this whole kingdom ; and may still succeed, if God doth not continue that public spirit, which He hath almost miraculously kindled in us upon this occasion.

Thus we see the public is many times, as it were, at the mercy of the meanest instrument, who can be wicked enough to watch opportunities of doing it mischief, upon the principles of avarice or malice, which I am afraid are deeply rooted in too many breasts, and against which there can be no defence, but a firm resolution in all honest men, to be closely united and active in showing their love to their country, by preferring the public interest to their present private advantage. If a passenger, in a great storm at sea, should hide his goods, that they might not be thrown overboard to lighten the ship, what would be the consequence? The ship is cast away, and he loses his life and goods together.

We have heard of men, who, through greediness of gain, have brought infected goods into a nation; which bred a plague, whereof the owners and their families perished first. Let those among us consider this and tremble, whose houses are privately stored with those materials of beggary and desolation, lately brought over to be scattered like a pestilence among their countrymen, which may probably first seize upon themselves and their families, until their houses shall be made a dunghill.

I shall mention one practice more, by which the meanest instruments often succeed in doing public mischief; and this is, by deceiving us with plausible arguments, to

T

make us believe that the most ruinous project they can offer is intended for our good, as it happened in the case so often mentioned. For the poor ignorant people, allured by the appearing convenience in their small dealings, did not discover the serpent in the brass, but were ready, like the Israelites, to offer incense to it ; neither could the wisdom of the nation convince them, until some, of good intentions, made the cheat so plain to their sight, that those who run may read. And thus the design was to treat us, in every point, as the Philistines treated Samson (I mean when he was betrayed by Delilah), first to put out our eyes, and then to bind us with fetters of brass.

I proceed to the last thing I proposed, which was to show you that all wilful injuries done to the public, are very great and aggravating in the sight of God.

First, It is apparent from Scripture, and most agreeable to reason, that the safety and welfare of nations are under the most peculiar care of God's providence. Thus He promised Abraham to save Sodom, if only ten righteous men could be found in it. Thus the reason which God gave to Jonah for not destroying Nineveh was, because there were six score thousand men in that city.

All government is from God, who is the God of
order ; and therefore whoever attempts to breed confusion or disturbances among a people, doth his utmost
to take the government of the world out of God's
hands, and to put it into the hands of the devil, who
is the author of confusion. By which it is plain, that
no crime, how heinous soever, committed against particular persons, can equal the guilt of him who does
injury to the public.

Secondly, All offenders against their country lie
under this grievous difficulty : that it is impossible to
obtain a pardon or make restitution. The bulk of
mankind are very quick at resenting injuries, and very
slow at forgiving them : and how shall one man be
able to obtain the pardon of millions, or repair the
injury he hath done to millions ? How shall those,
who, by a most destructive fraud, got the whole wealth
of our neighbouring kingdom into their hands, be ever
able to make a recompense ? How will the authors
and promoters of that villainous project, for the ruin
of this poor country, be able to account with us for
the injuries they have already done, although they
should no farther succeed ? The deplorable care of
such wretches must entirely be left to the unfathom-
able mercies of God : for those who know the least in

religion are not ignorant, that without our utmost endeavours to make restitution to the person injured, and to obtain his pardon, added to a sincere repentance, there is no hope of salvation given in the Gospel.

Lastly, All offences against our own country have this aggravation, that they are ungrateful and unnatural. It is to our country we owe those laws, which protect us in our lives, our liberties, our properties, and our religion. Our country produced us into the world, and continues to nourish us, so that it is usually called our mother ; and there have been examples of great magistrates, who have put their own children to death for endeavouring to betray their country, as if they had attempted the life of their natural parent.

Thus I have briefly shown you how terrible a sin it is to be an enemy to our country, in order to incite you to the contrary virtue, which at this juncture is so highly necessary, when every man's endeavour will be of use. We have hitherto been just able to support ourselves under many hardships ; but now the axe is laid to the root of the tree, and nothing but a firm union among us can prevent our utter undoing. This we are obliged to, in duty to our gracious King, as well as to ourselves.

Let us therefore preserve that public spirit, which God hath raised in us, for our own temporal interest. For, if this wicked project should succeed, which it cannot do but by our own folly ; if we sell ourselves for nought, the merchant, the shopkeeper, the artificer, must fly to the desert with their miserable families, there to starve, or live upon rapine, or at least exchange their country for one more hospitable than that where they were born.

Thus much I thought it my duty to say to you who are under my care, to warn you against those temporal evils which may draw the worst of spiritual evils after them ; such as heart-burnings, murmurings, discontents, and all manner of wickedness, which a desperate condition of life may tempt men to.

I am sensible that what I have now said will not go very far, being confined to this assembly ; but I hope it may stir up others of my brethren to exhort their several congregations, after a more effectual manner, to show their love for their country on this important occasion. And this, I am sure, cannot be called meddling in affairs of state.

I pray God protect his most gracious Majesty, and his kingdom long under his government ; and defend us from all ruinous projectors, deceivers, suborners perjurers, false accusers, and oppressors ; from the virulence of party and faction ; and unite us in loyalty to our King, love to our country, and charity to each other.